C000299181

The de Lafitte Protocol
No. 1

– JOHN VAN DEN BERGH –

An environmentally friendly book printed and bound in England by www.printondemand-worldwide.com

 **Mixed Sources**
Product group from well-managed forests, and other controlled sources
www.fsc.org Cert no. TT-COC-002641
© 1996 Forest Stewardship Council

 PEFC Certified
This product is from sustainably managed forests and controlled sources
www.pefc.org
PEFC/16-33-418

This book is made entirely of chain-of-custody materials

www.fast-print.net/store.php

THE DE LAFITTE PROTOCOL. No. 1.
Copyright © John van den Bergh 2014

A catalogue record for this book is available from the British Library

Back cover photograph of Oxford by Chris Andrews/Oxford Picture Library

ISBN 978-178456-134-5

First published 2014 by
FASTPRINT PUBLISHING
Peterborough, England.

*This saga thriller with its two sequels
(a trilogy) is dedicated to Marion and our 11
angels, who are the embodiment of every
nuance of goodness to be found therein.*

"As you read this thriller, completely immersed in the aristocratic milieu of hunt meets and private jets, you will be diverted by the counterpoint of the ex-Mafia family of hired gangsters stalking them with their Zeiss scopes and the Milanese silencers. You will be caught up with the sheer propulsive energy of the narrative, leaving you consistently entertained throughout."

Preface by John van den Bergh

I thought that the above slick press release proposed by a consultant editor did not adequately reflect the broader perspective in which the first book of this trilogy was written. Therefore, I would add the following.

The predominant memory I have of when I was three years old was hearing my mother one evening fervently reciting the rosary out loud in the hall of the chateau where I was born. There was also a note of alarm in her voice. She then indicated to me to go downstairs and sleep in the fortified cellars. It subsequently transpired that this was her manner of alluding to something to do with the rapid development of World War II.

Ever since then the so-called mysteries of both world wars have become so twisted by an endless supply of historians over so many years. These mysteries have been and are still, "On the cusp of it all being solved by yet more historians."

Now, in 2014 – to most of us of a non-atheistic persuasion – it is already abundantly clear that both wars, together with the atheistic Communist revolutions in Russia/China/Vietnam etc., accounted – in all – for the greatest loss of life of any century in history. The root cause, of course, was (and continues to be) blatant atheism. The most effective antidote is simplicity itself.

'But governments don't do God any more.' However, *Country Life* does. See that beautiful front cover of the September 24 2014 edition of a young English girl in rapt prayer (beside her eager terrier, which is intent on looking at her breakfast). It perfectly illustrates Mark Hedges's editorial "Priority is Peace".

In short, that is why I have devoted only three of the opening chapters of this trilogy to be set at the end of that atheistic century – if only to allude to the indomitable resistance to atheism. Too much has already been written about that century.

Thank God that humanity has recognised that there were still a few active Christian leaders in post-war Europe and the USA, i.e. Elizabeth II, Adenauer, de Gaulle, Salazar and Kennedy, who felt the shame of what had been allowed to occur.

Have all of us not been (and, somehow, are we not still being) neglectful in not exposing the greatest sin of all, Satan's sin of pride, to proliferate worldwide? What are we going to do about it in this new century? We have made a poor start by that (doubtless) retribution of September 11 2011 which we imposed on ourselves, since evil begets evil.

The saga thriller of the *The de Lafitte Protocol* trilogy, a microcosm of life, starts off (the no.1 book) as a classic mystery thriller. With the no.2 book it develops into an action thriller as the family try to reset their Protocol as they would wish, and the no. 3 book ends as a thrilling love story: in John Henry Newman's words, when "Heart speaks to heart".

Colin Dexter's comment on the front of book (No 1) hits the nail on the head: "An alarmingly intriguing read."

THE DE LAFITTE PROTOCOL

Chapter One

B efore the dawn chorus on Saturday 28 November 1999, towards the end of the twentieth century, snow covered the huge parklands of the Lafitte forest outside Paris. It was perfect weather for the day of the lawn meet of the staghounds (which were already being selected for the large hound van) as intermittently the forest rang alive with their hound music.

The chief whipper-in – a small cheerful man aptly named Petit – called each hound by name, urging them to be quiet.

"Ta gueule, toi."[1] The kennels were some distance from the stable block, which was in turn was 100 yards from Chateau Lafitte.

Comte Jacques de Lafitte, the fit septuagenarian, was already mounted: it was far earlier than was his custom but, as master of the staghounds, he had also insisted on acting as huntsman. He was still mulling over the disturbing contents of a fax from his Oxford-based nephew Charles, largely to do with that young man's premonitions of an assassination due to take place. But, unknown to him, he would also be one of the intended quarry today.

Comte Jacques de Lafitte slowly became aware that he was no longer on his own and heard his attractive Scottish guest, Annabelle state that she had to go home that evening.

---

[1] "Shut your gob"

"No. Do stay for the hunt ball tonight, Annabelle," Uncle Jacques pleaded. The handsome old bachelor continued with his plea. "My nephew Charles is prevented from coming over this morning as my field master but he intends to come over from Oxford for the hunt ball tonight, and I know he was looking forward to meeting you again."

Uncle Jacques might then have glimpsed a sudden change of colour in the alluring countenance of fair Annabelle, albeit slightly concealed by the navy netting fixed to her top hat. But perhaps her hurried response, delivered in a whispered cut-glass English accent with just a suggestion of a warm whimsical Scottish burr, might have distracted her uncle from her blushes.

"If only I'd received your kind invitation for tonight's hunt ball in time, Uncle Jacques," she said, finishing with an ever more brilliant smile. But was he seeing or listening to her?

* * *

In the middle of the forest, half a mile away from the ice-laden pond down which the hunted stags ultimately sought refuge, the eldest of the ex-Mafia triplet assassins shivered on the topmost overhanging branch of a massive evergreen Atlas cedar.

"It won't be long now," the eldest of the Tre Terzina assassins thought. He tried to control his shivering and rested his massive sniper rifle on the fork of the top branch, rubbing himself to keep warm. The oldest by five minutes of the Tre Terzina[2], Il Terzina – now a fifty-year-old ex-Mafia assassin – already felt frozen to the bone. He felt doubly miserable that he'd been separated from his younger triplets: they had been assigned the Oxford assassination that same day.

---

[2] Triplets

"The ex-Mafia don should not have separated us," he thought. "It'll bring bad luck." He grinned wickedly as he gritted his rotten teeth, which were chattering while he froze on top of his hideout. The wily old don had, however, insisted on a $1,000,000 deposit on The de Lafitte Protocol contract from the secret pezzonovante[3].

Il Terzina picked up his Italian copy of the famous Barrett rifle again. His older brother Il Perfetto had been given instructions by the crafty old don to order six exact copies (one for each of the family) for cash, at a huge discount. He gazed through the clear view of the Zeiss scope overlooking the frozen pond half a mile distant and felt confident, but was still haunted by the odd cry of the eager staghounds wanting to be released. He tried to remain calm, aware that they always had this unsettling effect on him however far away they were. But how would he cope once they were released from the hound van?

Earlier that same Saturday he'd been badly rattled when (only briefly) he'd caught their chilling hound music in the forest, while they'd started baying in their kennels during the initial selection process. Each hound was individually picked before being placed into the strongest pack of staghounds for the annual lawn meet.

* * *

Comte Jacques de Lafitte continued to linger in the two-toned green hall of the stable block near the chateau. His mind had switched back to the disturbing contents of that fax he'd earlier received from his Oxford nephew Charles Russell-Lafitte – not only about the young man's premonition of an imminent assassination but, more disturbingly, that he could not act as field master today.

---

[3] Big shot

But Annabelle's bright voice again interrupted his deep contemplation as she repeated herself. "If only I'd received your invitation for tonight's ball in time, Uncle Jacques."

"How has this once-gawky schoolgirl (whom he hadn't seen for 10 years) transformed herself into this exquisite young beauty?" Jacques wondered to himself. "And how wonderful that some girls still went to all the trouble of dressing up when riding side-saddle," he thought. Then he remembered fondly, having entertained another beautiful but distantly-related niece last year on his birthday. What was her name again? Dr Caroline? Wasn't she now working for a charity in Bogota? He'd only met her once before but oh, what a serene beauty: a truly gentle young girl, already a lady.

Perhaps it had been the yawn he had been trying to suppress while pronouncing Charles's name that had caused Annabelle to change colour. He'd immediately lowered his eyes so as not to embarrass her further and smiled, thinking how her blush was just like his own when at that age. "Bless her," he thought, as he became more entranced by her beauty.

Continuing his discourse, he said, "It was on this very day 222 years ago that a very distant ancestor of our family, Comte Alexis Orlov – with the help of just two servants – brought one of his grey yearling Orlov stallions and a young Orlov filly thousands of miles in a horsebox all the way from St Petersburg. Do you know he claimed later on that he'd been wrongly blamed for Napoleon's subsequent invasion of Moscow because he, Orlov, had first landed on French soil uninvited?"

The old man laughed, moving his mount closer to Annabelle's and admiring her radiant smile. He was dumbfounded by her beauty as she raised her veil to look at him with her features wide open with joy. Jacques's expression of admiration bounced back at him from the girl's pale, powder blue eyes, and now it was he who felt caught. He started searching for words.

"That's my Arab – no – Charles's Arab you've selected. You do remember him, don't you? Charles Russell-Lafitte." Caught off guard again, Annabelle widened her brilliant smile at him. She was determined not to blush this time. "I'm so pleased I was allowed to select Charles's fine Arab," she sang boldly.

That morning the head groom had told her that Monsieur le Comte had instructed him to saddle up any horse Annabelle took a liking to. But the fellow hadn't told her who the stallion belonged to, and she'd never thought to enquire. She continued speaking and smiling broadly at her uncle.

"Do you know, I've only ever met Charles once? It was when we were all still children, many years ago at Uncle Charlemagne's place. Is Charles still so very bossy?" she laughed playfully as she continued.

"Uncle Charlemagne put him in charge of all us children when we were staying at his chateau in Suvretta. Am I not correct in assuming Charles to be a very, very distant cousin? Yes, I would like to meet him again," she said, laughing once more as though to shrug it off.

But this time Jacques detected a more-than-distinctive note in that cut-glass voice, and smiled knowingly. "Yes, my dear. Distant enough," he thought. "You both are perfectly suitable for Charles," and he returned her smile.

* * *

It had been well past midnight when Jacques had arrived back from Paris the night before. Then before dawn those infernal *Sécurité* helicopters had swooped down over the 17th-century chateau, preventing him from going to sleep. That was when he'd noticed Charles's message on his private fax machine on the bedside table. It referred to an earlier email he'd never received about Charles's premonition of an assassination and the necessity of his absence that morning. It said that the Oxford college authorities insisted that Charles had to remain in Oxford to collect his D.Phil in Nuclear Sciences in person. Charles would regretfully not be able to act as usual as field master at the lawn meet that morning.

Jacques was displeased but said his morning prayers and dashed off to get himself kitted out for the stag hunt, telling himself all the while to remain cool – to forget everything except the hunt today: he would be serving as master of hounds and would also take on the huntsman's duties as well. But on top of all that, he had to make do without Charles as field master. Today of all days. He disliked any change in his routine.

* * *

The stag hunt had changed little from the first lawn meet, held back in 1778, to mark the occasion when Count Orlov had presented one of his rare handsome grey stallions and an Orlov filly as a surprise wedding gift to a distant de Lafitte relative.

* * *

Jacques now became anxious for Annabelle. It would be the first time that the young Arab would be out hunting since he'd given him to Charles last year. How could she - this slip of a girl - hope to handle the young stallion? He noted how the Arab's white sheen set off the flowing lines of her exquisite navy-blue hunting costume. "She's so ineffably beautiful," he thought, but then his thoughts were again on Charles as they switched back to the rumours of assassination, and his face set hard. Promptly his face brightened again as he remembered his duties as host.

Chapter Two

I t took Charles Russell-Lafitte a few puzzling moments in Oxford to come to grips with his nightmare (which he had just awoken from) and to realise he was not at his uncle's lawn meet outside Paris. He reached instinctively for the overhead switch. The instant light dazzled him but he jerked himself upright, stared bleary-eyed at the blue-striped wallpaper of his bedroom and looked for the Longines wristwatch given to him by his father. It showed 5.20 a.m.. His bearings began to seep into his consciousness. Of course. He was still at his father's house. Today he would have to go to the Sheldonian and collect his D.Phil.

* * *

Charles's father, Sir Basil Russell-Lafitte, a retired All Souls law don, had forsaken a career in his family's vast enterprises to pursue a more academic vocation, but he'd meanwhile counselled his son, indulging his love of St Thomas Aquinas. "Remember, always follow your own dreams, with 'Prudence, justice, fortitude and temperance'."

Accordingly, Charles had decided – many years later, when he was of age – to read for a doctorate in nuclear energy at Oxford. That way he might be able to contribute to his family's cutting-edge research and development role in nuclear technology and make a useful contribution to the family's billion-dollar Swiss foundation.

Charles frowned as he recalled he would be absent as field master for the stag hunt later that morning at Chateau Lafitte. Uncle Jacques would be master of hounds and, as usual, would also insist on being huntsman himself. But who would then be his field master? With that thought Charles recalled yesterday's inadequate email to his uncle, in which he'd apologised for not being able to fulfil his customary duty at the lawn meet.

But he had to remain in Oxford to collect in person an unusual gold medal – together with his D.Phil. – at the Sheldonian. But his troubled mind surged back to last night's nightmare of the assassination, a haunting fostered amid a feeling of dark foreboding about a former family friend, the ex-MI6 lawyer Sir Henry Steere. Was he not now involved with that last remaining ex-Mafia-planted Vatican bishop, Il Ciprioni?

Charles's disturbed thoughts were heightened, having recently read about the American Barrett sniper rifle with its pinpoint accuracy of over a mile. It was no use thinking about all this any further. He had to follow up yesterday's weak inconclusive email to Uncle Jacques with a more disturbing and unequivocal fax message now.

With a frown still wrinkling his high tanned forehead the Oxford rowing blue jumped down from his high 18th-century bed in his boxer shorts. Ignoring his leather slippers, he bolted across the modern carpet and flicked on the lights in the adjoining study-cum-dressing/exercise room. There, on a small antique desk, two black and white photographs of his distant cousins Caroline Conolly-Lafitte and the equally gawky Annabelle Beaumont (as young schoolgirls) caught his eye. "Yes," he thought, "I must arrange to meet them both again, and soon."

He switched on his old MacBook. Today's degree ceremony would be the culmination of many years of hard work, but first he must warn Uncle Jacques of the dramatic premonition that had just rendered him consciously aware of the danger he'd experienced. Feverishly, he redrafted his earlier email:

URGENT FAX 29.11.99.
This is an urgent confirmation fax.
Ref: yesterday's email to Comte Jacques de Lafitte.

Dear Uncle Jacques,

I deeply regret as per yesterday's email that I'll not be able to act as your field master today. College authorities insist on my having to collect my DPhil at the Sheldonian today, in person (something about sticking to the college rules today because they will be awarding some special medals).

NB I was awoken at 5.20 from a most disturbing nightmare. I'm sure it is a sort of premonition (no doubt following on from all those recent assassination warnings you've been receiving, discussed ad nauseam in the past, thought you persist in dismissing them) ... Do take extra care today, please.

While I instinctively agree with your uneasy feelings concerning Sir Henry Steere, there's nothing we can prove as yet. Also, that ex-Mafia-planted bishop, Il Ciprioni, is a dangerous fellow (from the little I've heard about him). We'll discuss it again tonight at the hunt ball.

Safe hunting, meanwhile, and give my love to Cousin Annabelle.

Love, Charles R-L.

Charles blessed himself, settled himself on one of the Ergo rowing machines and watched the printed copy's text as it came off the printer. Running his muscular hand through his tousled hair, he read it over again – especially the references to Sir Henry and the dubious prelate Ciprioni, which he'd forgotten to highlight. He again started to transfer a copy of that text to his fax machine and dispatched his message to his uncle's private fax number at the chateau. He smiled as he remembered Uncle Jacques asking him last year to silence the ringtone on the simple fax machine he'd given him for Christmas, so that it would not wake him. It was still probably beside his uncle's four-poster at the chateau. With that thought Charles blessed himself again before mounting the adjoining running machine, and said an interior prayer.

"Lord, you know my exercises come second to my prayers to you – but I'm simply combining two operations, as time is precious now." He then commenced running at speed and silently mouthed five decades of the rosary with his morning prayers, checking the fax machine's connection as he ran. He knew from timing himself in the past that after the fifth decade his half-hour of running would be complete. Halfway through he increased his running speed before finally pushing the slow down and stop button. He blessed himself once more after the vigorous exercise, slipped the sheet of paper into an open tray marked "Private", stretched, undressed and took a shower.

* * *

Mid morning, Charles sat dutifully waiting with his fellow graduates in the gigantic hall of the Sheldonian in Oxford. He was still regretting having had to miss the thrill of the annual lawn meet, but consoled himself that at least he'd collected his degree and the unusual Oxford gold medal for excellence.

It felt heavy in his hand as he examined it, together with its long blue ribbon. He hoped to get away promptly (the sooner the better) to catch the Eurostar train to Paris, so as to be in good time for the hunt ball that night. But last night's trauma had taken its toll and (as the degree ceremony continued to drag on) Charles closed his sleepy eyes – allowing his mind to switch back to the Lafitte forest outside Paris, alive with hound music and the clarion calls of French horns.

But as he indulged himself in this pastoral dream, those searing images of his nightmare soon broke into his consciousness again. Again there was that dramatic blast of the assassin's powerful rifle which, combined with the additional noise and confrontation of his fellow graduates standing up loudly at the conclusion of the protracted degree ceremony, woke him up. He was completely shattered … he and his fellow graduates surged en bloc towards the eastern exit door of the Sheldonian.

As his scarlet doctoral gown billowed in the cold college winds he looked up and thought he saw a shadow at Hertford Bridge (popularly known as the Bridge of Sighs). Just as his left shoe was about to touch the middle of the worn-down hollow of the second stone step, a camera-clutching tourist called out, "Can you swing the medal up higher? Right up, please." Charles looked around without stopping, obliging with good humour, and swung up the gold medal for excellence as far as it would go – and then laughed at the unaccountable embarrassment he felt.

All at once he sensed something strike the gold medal as the blue ribbon was forced from his hand. He heard a twang as a bullet – faster than the speed of sound – deflected from the gold medal and plunged into his back with a blinding pain, keeling him over, while a prayer flashed through his mind, "Oh, my God. Let me live."

The Oxford University Bulldogs (police) were promptly on the scene that Saturday. When they drew a blank they reacted quickly and called in Scotland Yard, who in turn consulted MI5, who promptly involved MI6.

As the significance of the de Lafitte family quickly became known to the security services they called in the CIA, who duly roped in Interpol – to no avail – as the mystery continued to overwhelm them all. Meanwhile Charles was rushed to the nearest hospital, where doctors discovered a silver bullet lodged dangerously close to his spine.

Sir Basil Russell-Lafitte was determined to seek out the best possible surgeon for his only son and heir. So he promptly left for the countryside to seek out his trusty fishing companion, a former surgeon, whose advice was swift and to the point.

"No … don't go near your local professor, whatever you do," said his best friend. "He knows everything, but it's his hands. No: appoint his young assistant, the South African. They say he's also a brilliant violinist." But would it save Charles's life, or would he be bedridden for the rest of his life as a paraplegic?

Chapter Three

That same day in France Uncle Jacques continued to pronounce "Cousin Anna-belle," with his strong French accent emphasising the belle part of her name. "Charles faxed me this morning. Never got his email. They're still so unreliable, don't you think? Charles was full of apologies, saying he couldn't get out of being present in Oxford today in person, to receive his D.Phil. His father told me he'd be receiving a special gold medal for his dissertation on nuclear energy."

Jacques the bachelor smiled proudly, as if Charles was his own son. But he received no comment, just a huge beam of delight from Annabelle, and continued, "He's never missed a lawn meet before, you know." Finding it tiresome to have to try to camouflage his disappointment on receipt of that fax, he thought, "How will it be possible to control all those hunt members without the presence of my favourite nephew acting as my field master?" But then he added aloud, "No, that's not strictly accurate. He was absent once before, more than 10 years ago, when he was keeper of the wall game. That was a very special day for him and, in my book, a legitimate excuse … not an excuse at all, really … because he was fulfilling his duty as keeper to his school and his team."

Jacques hoped he'd not become too serious as they rode out of the long 17th-century stable block side by side. But as he became resolutely silent, he frowned as master when he caught the fragrance of Annabelle's Givenchy III perfume. He, however, overcame his censure and duly smiled with pleasure that she had chosen that particular brand – always a favourite of the family and his wide circle of friends.

He pointed vigorously with his hunting crop at the large group of mounted hunters already gathered in front of the chateau. "Look at the splendid turnout," he said, smiling broadly. With that, a pleasing thought brightened his mood still further. "That's it," he thought, suddenly finding the answer to an earlier concern.

"Annabelle, I've just had this thought – a solution to a serious problem which has been nagging me all morning. I've decided, as of now, that I'm making you my acting field master, instead of Charles. I'm also insisting you'll stay on for tonight's hunt ball, too, instead of going back to be marooned in the wilds of Scotland."

Annabelle winced, but she could see Uncle Jacques was already treating it as a fait accompli, as he continued in that deadpan tone of voice of his (which he used when he'd made an irreversible decision).

"Nothing to it, really," he added. "Just make sure the horses don't crowd the hounds. Do it with the full confidence and authority I've just given you as my new field master." When he looked away, as he did, she concluded there was be no room for any further discussion. So she laughed, attempting to hide her concern about taking on this extra responsibility, teasing him instead about his reference to Scotland. "I would not trade the Highlands for anything, ever. But I'll gladly stay on for tonight's hunt ball, if only to please you, Uncle Jacques." Taken by her quick wit, he helpfully added, "I'm sure the chambermaid will fix you up with one of the many ball gowns hanging about." He grinned as he nonchalantly gestured to one of the passing trays. Inviting her to take a stirrup cup – and taking one himself – he raised his glass and added, "Let's drink to that, and good hunting."

As they mingled with the main body of horses Jacques beamed with good cheer as he greeted the hunt members all around in French. "Good morning," he said. Receiving greetings from all sides, he continued to observe Annabelle with fascination. He watched her switch her eyes to some riders sitting astride their horses, English style. Some of them were already replacing their empty stirrup cups back on to the passing trays before urging each other to take further stirrup cups.

Jacques chuckled and then began to wonder ... Should he tell her about the speech he was going to make tonight at the ball, bequeathing the chateau and its grounds to Charles? No. It would keep. After all, he'd no particular reason for telling her – although she was clearly Charles's ideal chatelaine. "No," he thought, "Must be sensible. Must keep my promise to my brother Basil to stay out of Charles's private life at all times. He's only 27. Mustn't start meddling. But he'd better not remain a bachelor like me. He'd regret not having a son. Nor wait till he's 40, like brother Basil, before he ties the knot. Tonight she'll be reintroduced to Charles at the ball by yours truly."

Then, as master and huntsman, he gave his signal to the French horns, who sounded their rousing clarion calls – to which the staghounds responded with their own excited music, signalling as a pack that they were now eager to be sent into the first covert as soon as the master himself sounded his own hunting horn. Annabelle kept a short distance behind Uncle Jacques and made sure she controlled the rest of the field, after they had first released a boxed stag.

* * *

By the middle of the day, after some exciting gallops, Jacques allowed his de Lafitte pack of hounds to switch their line to the strong scent of an outlier stag. With that the music of the staghounds changed to a shrill yapping combined with excited howling, amid the thrill and excitement of the whole field running at full stretch.

No one noticed the hidden ex-Mafia assassin camouflaged at the top of the tall evergreen cedar, while his mobile phone vibrated silently with a vital text in Italian: "Abort all killings instantly. *Omertà*." The eldest of the ex-Mafia Tre Terzina triplets froze when he received that message, and suspected that his younger triplets had made a mess of it in Oxford. "There'll be a hell of a price to pay for this," he thought. "I warned them not to rely on Osama bin Laden student's memory of when he was in Oxford as a boy."

* * *

After a wild but exciting hunt, accounting for only that one outlier stag, it was late in the evening – after everyone had bathed – that the horrific news could just be contained among family members at the chateau: "Charles has been shot in Oxford."

Still in his dressing room, Jacques went pale with shock. "*Pauvre Charles*," he thought, reconciling himself to the certainty that Charles would not be arriving that evening after all. His own retirement would have to be put on hold again. He'd have to reword his speech for tonight's ball, but in honour of Charles he'd retain the news and refuse to cancel the ball. What would he say now to Annabelle? "I've never been a success at matchmaking," he thought. "It's in the hands of the Lord now, where it should of course remain."

But he'd make it his business to find out who and what was driving all this. "Must read Charles's fax again," he thought – and blessed himself carefully, thinking, "What new surprises will the new millennium bring the de Lafitte family?" He fell to his knees and prayed, remembering the saying of the South

American cardinal Jorge Mario, "Only love can save us." And then out loud to Our Lady, asking her to protect the family.

"Hail Mary, full of grace. The Lord is with thee. Blessed art thou among women and blessed is the fruit of thy womb, Jesus. Holy Mary, mother of God, pray for us sinners now and at the hour of our death. Amen."

Refreshed, he now stood up and prepared himself for dinner and the ball.

The cook and the kitchen staff had been busy all day, preparing for a buffet dinner before the ball that evening. Before the eight o'clock gong in the hall sounded Uncle Jacques went into the library and explained to the family members that, in honour of Charles, he'd decided that the last thing Charles would have wanted was the cancellation of the last hunt ball of the century. "The show must go on would have been Charles's wish," said Uncle Jacques to loud applause. So the family members present in the library raised their champagne glasses to him for a speedy recovery. Then he summoned the other 75 hunt members for drinks in the hall and adjoining dining room.

The stalwarts of the hunting community were evenly matched by the large number of overseas de Lafitte family members. Marc de Beaumont from Switzerland was greeting his cousins, aunts and uncles – warmly bringing regrets for the absence of his father Charlemagne, the Duc de Beaumont and his wife. But he turned white with shock when he heard that his best friend Charles had been shot while coming out of the degree ceremony outside the Sheldonian. He quickly blessed himself. "Oh, my God," he'd uttered, astonished, wondering what he could do to help. Marie St Julien, also from Switzerland, comforted Marc and Annabelle – who soon brought good cheer from all their other relations from France, the UK, Ireland, Germany, Austria, the USA, New Zealand, Australia and Scotland.

After a formal grace was said by the local parish priest at about 10 p.m. the huge double door leading to the ballroom was thrown open and the young village orchestra struck up their band with gusto. Soon the various languages melded smoothly with a traditional waltz followed by jazz and even Beatles music – which blended well with the village orchestra's pop melodies, adding joy all around deep into the night.

The senior members toddled off to their allocated bedrooms upstairs – or down a further set of stairs, off to their respective transport and local domiciles. Most of the younger members who'd travelled from afar chose to stay upstairs in huge dormitories of bunk beds and sleeping bags, rather than go off to adjoining chateaux.

Plans were already being hatched for the forthcoming new-century ball to be held in the village square under extended marquees. Uncle Jacques, as honorary mayor of the village – together with the parish priest – announced that they would welcome lots of help to their ad hoc committee.

Chapter Four

A dozen years later the ex-MI6 lawyer/killer Sir Henry Steere was scheming away, as was his custom, in his first floor office of the NYPB (the New York Private Bank). It had taken him more than a decade to have insinuated himself into the executive chairmanship of the NYPB – formerly a subsidiary of de Lafitte America, and now a semi-dormant institution that his grandparents had been given as former loyal stewards by the de Lafitte family in the USA. So many banks had meanwhile collapsed and now, towards the close of 2011, there seemed little prospect of improvement in 2012.

The lanky old man shuddered. It had taken every ounce of his guile to persuade his tame auditors with the previous year's accounts, but how much longer could he survive for? Sir Henry now felt even more desperate than when he had instigated The de Lafitte Protocol more than 12 years ago.

But now that he was fully in control he decided he could reactivate his earlier plan properly, but this time without any involvement of al-Qaeda. His plan would continue to be dubbed The de Lafitte Protocol. But unlike 12 years ago – when he'd been rushed and not fully in control and it went so horribly wrong, they'd get it right this time around. Now they'd dispensed with Osama bin Laden's earlier unwelcome Oxford involvement. This time he had all the Italian ex-Mafia don's specialist ex-Mafia killers on board, in particular Il Perfetto, who'd never missed completing a contract.

The oldest son of the ex-don had been excused from participating in the Oxford contract for reasons not entirely clear. Another touch of blackmail would be required to get to the bottom of it all: greasing the palm of the ex-don had done wonders. But now that he knew about the ex-don's bastard son Il Ciprioni, already a bishop in the Vatican, it had opened up a new ball game. As he had done 12 years ago, he would again officially retire – and tonight was the designated time when he would host another farewell banquet for another batch of directors.

"This time we'll get it right," he thought. He was confident that they would succeed this time, but was somewhat surprised that he had found it necessary to repeat his thought process about Il Perfetto, the ex-Mafia don's eldest son. Anyhow, the ex-Mafia don had given his assurance that Il Perfetto would be put in charge of liquidating the entire de Lafitte clan, thereby enabling Sir Henry to be nominated as the new chairman of the cash-rich de Lafitte nuclear company, *Aligoté Nucléaire SA*. And then to hell with all those expensive and time-consuming safety standards the de Lafittes had always insisted on conforming to. Once he'd got control of their wealth-creating machine he could save his bank and excavate for himself the cash reserves they had locked up, with the huge financial bonus of more than $1 billion dollars on top.

With that thought he selected another Cuban cigar, opened the secret file he'd taken from a secure safe located in the wall behind him and started to read the headlines from a copy of the *Sunday Morning* dated 29 November 1999. He read again the headline, starkly printed against the now-yellowing paper:

"*GRADUATE OF 27 GUNNED DOWN!*" below a photograph of the stricken graduate lying on the cobblestones outside the Sheldonian, the short article continued:

Robed in a scarlet doctoral gown with silk taffeta facings, the gold-medal graduate lies spreadeagled on grey cobblestones outside Wren's Sheldonian. In the foreground some fellow graduates can be seen kneeling over the victim. Some are clinging on to their mortar boards while others, with open mouths, are screaming. Earlier, a camera-clutching tourist had urged, "Can you swing it up higher?" referring to the gold medal encircled at the top right-hand corner of the photograph in which a dent is clearly visible.

It is speculated this medal deflected the bullet away from the graduate's head and into his body, paralysing him. "A high-flyer: a rowing blue" was how one of his fellow graduates described him.

None of the authorities in Oxford had been able to account for the shooting, even when Scotland Yard had been called in. None of the statements made to the Oxford bulldogs that afternoon seemed to shed any light on the matter. Dr Charles Russell-Lafitte's name had been kept out of the news media's orbit. Instead, a spurious mention had been made at that time that one of the skylight windows of Blackwell's bookshop (overlooking Christopher Wren's rotunda on Broad Street) had been ajar at the time of the shooting, but this was eventually discounted as having no possible implications. Sir Henry smiled cynically, replacing the yellowing newspaper cut-out.

He then removed the top secret memo – obtained all those years ago from one of his previous contacts in MI6 – that lay underneath. It read:

Urgent Action: Send duplicate of this memo to the CIA in the normal manner. *Is there something in the assertion that Osama bin Laden might have been involved? His presence in Oxford around that time is apparent from a photograph of a large number of the bin Laden family standing outside an Oxford language school* (from an earlier copy of *The Oxford Times*.)

Sir Henry dragged on his cigar while he recalled the tricky situation at that time. As soon as he'd learned that the Oxford assassination had failed he had immediately instructed the ex-Mafia don to cease all operations, though it had proved impossible to stop the Chinese assassination. In time this had been interpreted as a genuine accident, anyway. But at least a message had reached the Tre Terzina assassin in time, while he was perched on top of the huge cedar tree in the Lafitte forest during the annual stag hunt. So the whole story eventually died down. Everything was quiet now. No one had even hinted of a wider plot behind the foul play. If they had, the finger would have pointed at al-Qaeda anyhow.

But this time Sir Henry had made sure they were no longer involved. Sir Henry closed the file, locking it away in the safe again. He leaned back in his armchair and blew some smoke rings. "Make haste slowly," he thought. That's exactly what he'd done. But dramatic progress was now – finally – going to be made, following on from tonight's press release.

Sir Henry looked out of the window. The snow was thick on the ground that Saturday evening in late November 2011. He was scheming again, and thought he'd just put his head next door to see how the adjoining boardroom – expensively decked out for dinner for another batch of non-executive directors – looked.

"They'll arrive soon," he thought. He checked his father's gold pocket watch. "Nearly 20.00 hours. Another four long hours of nonsense tonight," he thought. He sighed and opened the adjoining double door a further fraction.

"I must remain calm and relaxed at all times," he reminded himself as he heard the bell of the main door downstairs.

"That's them." He quickly sought an ashtray. "Where's Mac? Where's the champagne?"

Chapter Five

A fter a lavish five-course dinner, Saturday night merged into the small hours of the last Sunday of November 2011. The non-executive directors of the NYPB thanked their host. "They're doing it too profusely again," Sir Henry thought. He was feeling impatient, as it was already past midnight and he was expecting a vital phone call from Geneva. One by one the directors trooped out of the long, richly-panelled room, each varying marginally the classic platitudes on Sir Henry's retirement. "Well deserved, Harry," or "Good luck this time," they said.

This farewell resignation dinner was even more puzzling than the first one he'd given 12 years ago. It too had been considered over the top, but the opulence of tonight's event was especially glaring after the collapse of the many banks in the past few years and months.

The vice president's regular secretary, Betty, had just gone on holiday. Now a gap year student was peering outside through the muslin curtains at Betty's window, apparently keen and excited about her current work experience assignment. She'd clearly ignored Betty's warning about the bank's dress code: her new black shoes and tight yellow hip-hugging trousers stood out against the well-worn, faded red carpet of Betty's office. Technically it was already Sunday morning by her watch. She stared at the directors down below, who were climbing into their extended limousines before being driven away.

Once they'd disappeared she picked up a copy of the revised press release she'd been given by Betty earlier on Friday and took it into the cigar smoke-filled boardroom. Mac, her boss – a former senior clerk and now a vice president of the bank – read it quickly before dismissing the girl with an irritating movement of his fat little finger. Unconscious of the drunken tone of his voice, he addressed his only remaining companion – the chairman of the bank, Sir Henry Steere. "This'll give you the cover you're looking for, Harry." It was a false familiarity: both men instantly knew it.

Mac slid the A4 paper awkwardly across the smooth mahogany dining table towards Sir Henry – who proceeded to ignore it, refusing to face the blatant dishonesty behind his own press release. Throughout dinner Sir Henry had overheard some of Mac's half phrases and slurred words, which only confirmed his long-held suspicions that Mac probably pretended to know more than he actually did. But what if it wasn't pretence? Suppose the bastard actually knew the whole truth? Sir Henry peered at him again from underneath his heavily-lidded eyes. Annoyed, he looked at his watch again, still deliberately ignoring the press release. But he leaned forward and very slowly selected another cigar from the ebony box standing within reach. He lit up a large Montecristo, blowing clouds of rich smoke into Mac's drunken face, then surreptitiously scanned the document. It read:

Press Release New York, Sat 26 Nov 2011. The board of the NYPB (New York Private Bank, formerly the de Lafitte-Steere Bank) gave a farewell dinner as a mark of honour to the retiring chairman, Sir Henry Steere. The occasion marks the 12-year postponement in the 77-year-old's retirement as president. Sir Henry will be retiring to Kentucky, where he has accepted his appointment as joint master of the Gordonston Hunt.

The beginnings of a cruel smirk flickered across Sir Henry's lips. Mac must surely be aware that games were again being played. But the fellow couldn't know – not even after 20 years of trying to figure it all out – the purpose of these games. It was a stupid trick, really – one that Sir Henry had picked up while working at MI6, long before he took over the bank from his father. "Always keep them guessing," his father had urged him. Combine that with over-the-top drunken buffoonery and no one would ever suspect one of anything serious. He now cast his hard eyes on Mac, who was seated but falling asleep. Sir Henry's sharp weather-beaten face bristled with annoyance. Why hadn't the de Lafitte's Swiss lawyer phoned? Was there another problem? Again? Damn. He'd just have to wait and be patient a little longer. As he leaned back in his leather chesterfield at the head of the table he gave way to a silent laugh, revealing a full row of surprisingly large yellow teeth that were normally hidden by his immaculate silver moustache. "Excellent press release," he thought. "------- good smokescreen."

Mac suddenly let out a loud snore. Sir Henry looked across at him. "The ------- fool," he thought. "He must be suffering from sleep apnoea." Sir Henry half decided he would have to deal with Mac himself, even before he left this building today. "Can't afford to let the fellow jeopardise our crucial operations after all these years," he thought.

Yet again he lifted his pocket watch from his waistcoat and looked at the crystal face, calculating ... It must be five o'clock in France. The planned disruption of the electronic networks down the entire eastern seaboard of the US would not have gone into effect yet. It would affect communications with Europe for possibly two full days – perhaps even 10 days. But one short weekend was all Sir Henry needed. Again he congratulated himself on his insistence that al-Qaeda be excluded henceforth, following that incompetent fiasco in Oxford in 1999.

Sir Henry blew another perfect smoke ring and watched its change of colour from blue to grey to tan before floating away, becoming larger and larger. Mac seemed more circumspect of late, but surely he couldn't have found out about a renewed attempt at mass murder? Sir Henry felt the build-up of moisture in his moustache, which was a foolproof warning that he was becoming worried.

"We need a bit of tomfoolery," he decided, and jumped up from his chair, spilling the contents of the brandy glass over his black pinstriped trousers. "Bloody hell," he roared at the top of his voice, as the crystal beaker shattered against one of the tripod end supports of the early 19th-century table legs. "Bloody hell," he roared again at the top of his voice, kicking a row of empty chairs for added confusion.

Mac woke up and rushed forward apologetically to assist Sir Henry – who indicated with his outstretched forefinger that he wanted to make for the large fireplace, the only one in Wall Street still allowed to burn wood. Sir Henry looked up at the huge mantelpiece of white marble and proceeded to dangle from it, displaying wet trouser bottoms with legs akimbo in front of the dying embers. He was puffing furiously on his big cigar when suddenly the preppy-sounding voice of Mac's replacement secretary rang out from the speakerphone.

"Sir, there's a personal call for Sir Henry Steere from Geneva. The caller refuses to give his name and, sir, he says he's calling from a payphone. He wants to know if we will collect the call, and would I switch on the scrambler?" Mac hastened back to the table, turned off the speakerphone and then picked up the receiver.

"Yes to that last request and yes, put him through." He turned to the chairman. "Harry," he whispered loudly, "Isn't that the call you've been waiting for?" Sir Henry frowned. What did Mac's conspiratorial tone of voice suggest? He turned his head slowly, peering distrustfully at Mac through the heavy cigar smoke. That fellow might indeed know too much. Perhaps he had somehow heard of the plan to crash all communications along the eastern seaboard. Could he also have found out about the pending assassinations?

Slowly Sir Henry lowered his legs down to the floor and carefully removed his pale hands from the mantelpiece, throwing his unfinished cigar into the embers of the fire as he affected to stagger back slowly to the dining table. But his mind was working at speed. "Surely the fellow doesn't know about the ex- Mafia Bishop, Il Ciprioni? Could he? Never mind how. Damn. I must deal with Mac before it's too late," he thought.

"Switch on the scrambler and put him through," Sir Henry barked. Mac held the receiver out to him. "He'll always be a clerk," Sir Henry decided. "A needlessly dangerous one too. Must take care of him this morning before he spills the beans." When Sir Henry approached the table he looked straight into Mac's small drunken green eyes. Not bothering to hide his contempt, he grabbed the receiver and turned his back on him. "Surely the fellow is still ignorant of what is about to befall the de Lafitte family," he thought. "Or is he just trying to be clever? No, no. I can't afford to take any risks. No more stupid risks." With that Sir Henry sank into his chesterfield at the head of the table.

"Hello? Sir Henry Steere here … *Herr Doctor* … So good of you to call, dear boy." He listened carefully to the clipped, mechanical Swiss voice clicking through the receiver. "We made the second payment last week to the Italian family, *ja*?" Dr Humburger's staccato voice sounded like a speaking clock. "They were told to commence the operation in one hour's time, *ja*? The signal activating the US communications failure will be sent at the same time." Sir Henry began to perspire but caught the mood, as he said, "Excellent, dear boy," and then waited for further news from Dr Humburger. "I will not ring again until Sunday night, when the communications system will be restored. Everything should be completed by then, anyhow. *Ja?*"

Sir Henry relaxed. "I look forward to that, *Herr Doctor*. Goodbye. I await your confirmation by the agreed coded email." Sir Henry waited for the click but he heard nothing. He sensed the Swiss lawyer was still on the line, and felt uneasy that his own drunken slur had been detected. Why had Humburger not made his usual derogatory comments today about the evils of excessive alcohol?

Sir Henry placed his long thin hand on his brow and nervously, gingerly, replaced the moist handset. No. No games today. It was his last chance to save his bank. Only then did he notice Mac's drunken green eyes burning into him. Sir Henry instantly squared up his shoulders military fashion, and with his right index finger brushed the underside of his moist silver moustache. "Good news. Yes … good news indeed," Sir Henry exclaimed. He invented as he waffled. His voice became loud and authoritative as he lied. "The loan collateral is finally coming through." He lied with the habitual fluency of a lawyer, not forgetting to look straight into Mac's eyes. "I'll have further news after the weekend."

With that, preparing his victim for his fate, he stood up and shook Mac's hand vigorously. "Thank you, dear boy, for staying up with me. It's so kind of you." There was a puzzled look on Mac's face as Sir Henry sailed out of the room before purposefully stopping at the double door to switch off the main chandelier. Mac in turn switched off each of the 16 wall lights along the bank's dining room, seeking comfort and taking delight in demonstrating to his boss the prudence of the thrifty banker he'd become.

It was in the ensuing darkness, as he stepped on to the landing, that Sir Henry confronted the enormity of his imminent acts of murder and betrayal. Dealing with Mac now would be the easy part, but how could he steel himself to carry out the killing of his dearest friend Senator Gordonston-Lafitte? Sir Henry's heavily-hooded eyes moistened and glistened in the semi-darkness. Each murderous act must proceed in precise detail, one after the other. There was no other way. Each act of butchery would lead to the next until the total plan was complete.

He switched on the balcony lights and the wall lights leading down the sweeping marble staircase and consulted his watch again. "The time difference with Europe and the international nature of the assassinations will make the killings more remote – and therefore, perhaps more bearable," he thought. He twitched nervously as Mac's pert temporary secretary suddenly came out of her adjoining office. He quickly handed her the press release. She accepted the page eagerly, still bright-eyed and keen for any work experience in New York, and retired back behind her door to make copies.

Sir Henry walked towards the giant staircase and looked down through the mock Regency banisters, assessing the dizzy spiral drop. "Yes, that should take care of Mac. That should overcome our little problem," he thought. He took another half step forward, both feet now at the very edge of the topmost white marble step. His eyes hardened, their hard impersonal gaze becoming that of an MI6 killer.

With his left hand firmly gripping the top of the mahogany banisters he swivelled round as he heard Mac closing the door of the dining room behind him. Beckoning Mac with an inviting smile to come to him he held up his right arm as if seeking support from Mac, and whispered urgently when he came alongside. "Be careful, Mac. Your shoelace is undone."

Mac bent down, vainly trying to focus his tired, drunken eyes and wondering which of his shoes Sir Henry was referring to.

Sir Henry's right hand – quicker than a heron's bill going for a fish – struck down on the back of Mac's neck with a karate chop,. The blow was calculated not to leave a mark, just sufficient to catch Mac off balance. The vice president tumbled head first down the steep marble steps to his death.

Chapter Six

In Oxford a telephone call from Paris furrowed Sir Basil Russell-Lafitte's pale brow. It was the eve of the 2011 lawn meet to be held at Chateau Lafitte, 12 years on from the 1999 event that had brought the devastating news of Charles's shooting.

Father and son were both at their modest estate overlooking Oxford. In the intervening years Sir Basil had continued to worry about his only son and heir, enlisting more teams of doctors … until one of them, a member of a very large family, persuaded him to take an active role in his son's daily exercises. Every day they continued, while a top security firm monitored the black wrought-iron gates at the front lodge of their estate. Through their chosen daily routines father and son became still closer. They blessed each other with Lourdes water every day – particularly after the terror unleashed on September 11 2001, which only served to strengthen their bond with the wider world community.

Sir Basil passed the receiver to his son after a quarter of an hour. "Charles … my brother Jacques for you." Charles listened, thinking how strange his uncle's voice sounded. "Charles, we've finally got a lead. Your shooting was indeed part of a larger plot of assassinations, as was the murder of Guy and his wife in China on the same day. We have new evidence about their so-called cable car accident. Do you really want to come over for the lawn meet tomorrow?"

"But I was determined to come over, Uncle Jacques." Charles spoke quietly but purposefully, firmly gripping the wooden handlebars of his crutches. "Transport has already been organised. We've always hunted together. I'm not letting you down 12 years in a row. Did you not receive the special saddle I sent over last week?"

"Yes, I did. Thank you."

There was a brief hesitation before Jacques continued. "Come over early, then – tomorrow morning, for breakfast. Our security people are insisting on coming out, too." Jacques's voice changed back to the normal tones of a benevolent uncle. "Charles, I'll instruct the head groom to put your special saddle on one of my steady Orlov horses."

"I'm sure I'll manage to stay on," Charles laughed encouragingly. "Hmm. Yes, that'll be helpful. It'll be good to have you back, Charles."

Jacques sincerely meant those words. The two of them had always hunted together until the Oxford shooting: their lawn meets had truly been red-letter days.

Feeling completely at home on his crutches, Charles reassured his uncle. "Actually, recently I've been cub hunting with the Kildares in Ireland. You know I was really looking forward to riding your generous gift. Remember the Arab yearling you kindly gave me 13 years ago?"

"Oh, he's a wild one," Jacques tut-tutted, laughing, ""I'll tell you later. Bye."

Uncle Jacques's sense of humour always cheered Charles up, but deep inside he began to feel apprehensive. So his shooting was part of a wider assassination plot, after all. And if Uncle Guy and Aunty Anne had been murdered in China, as Jacques claimed, who was behind their killing? Whoever it was, it confirmed Charles's worst suspicions: that someone was trying to kill off the whole de Lafitte family. Even Uncle Jacques, who had so readily dismissed all assassination threats in the past, sounded worried now — and was taking this new information seriously. But why was Jacques still afraid for Charles? Who would want to kill a severely disabled person now?

Sir Basil was at one with his son's concerns and, seeing how late it was, said, "Goodnight. We will not discuss it now, Charles. Let's sleep on it. Leave it till morning, before you leave for Paris."

Chapter Seven

In New York Sir Henry Steere watched Mac tumble down the marble steps and thought, "There's no way he could have survived that." But he had to be sure, and he slowly descended the pristine marble staircase until he came to the spot where the marble slabs became wider and bloodstained. He looked down coldly at the rumpled remains of his vice president. Mac was beyond help now, his neck broken after he had tumbled head first down those sharp steps and then had smashed into the curved wall.

Sir Henry's own narrow features had temporarily lost their ruddy colour. In the ancient narrow mirrors set into the wall lights of the staircase his weather-beaten skin now appeared moist, cold and slimy grey. He stood still, thinking, and lost all track of time. What had brought him to this? The de Lafitte family had started their first US bank with several of Sir Henry's ancestors as trustworthy managers. The de Lafittes kept a very low profile, but slowly and steadily acquired a large stake in Wall Street and –together with the Morgans and the Rockefellers – controlled a large chunk of Chicago and San Francisco through their Swiss foundation.

With the outbreak of World War II the de Lafittes had reorganised their worldwide holdings and even transferred their USA bank's licence to Sir Henry's ancestors. They'd even thrown in the original bank's Wall Street building – and with it the contents of its ancient vaults – to those devout Quakers. It was the very building in which Sir Henry had just killed his faithful personal assistant, Mac.

"Damn it," Sir Henry cursed quietly. He'd no way of knowing the full foolishness of the direction taken 12 years ago. Those ex-Mafia assassins involving al-Qaeda. What a fiasco. But now at last those ex-Mafia Italian bastards were finally united. Their best shooter, Il Perfetto, was on board at last – together with his abducted son, Il Ragazzo – whom he'd kidnapped at a maternity ward as a baby 39 years ago and who was now following in his father's footsteps as a sharpshooter.

Sir Henry decided that he would retain the title The de Lafitte Protocol. He refused to be associated with that dastardly word assassination: the killing of all that family was a forgone conclusion, but he liked the Comte de Lafitte, Sir Basil and – in particular – Senator Cecil and his son George. It had never been a personal matter: it was just that they were in the way of his ambition. Protocol had the ring of gravitas, which perfectly matched his ambition.

Before the Oxford disaster 12 years ago Sir Henry had made no comment at all about the proposed schedules of the assassinations. But on the same day of the Oxford fiasco everything had had to be instantly cancelled, which had been achieved by the ex-Mafia don enforcing the code of *omertà*. Sir Henry had then bribed the de Lafitte trustee lawyer in Geneva Dr Humburger into compliance with his plan, which gave him access to all Humburger's real-time inside information about the family and all its offshore non-domiciled activities. It should have been a doddle but for the idea of the intrusion of al-Qaeda replacing the ex-don's eldest son, Il Perfetto.

Dr Humburger was now Sir Henry's sole point of contact. Sir Henry wanted no interaction either with the assassins or the plotters. No one should now know of his existence at all. Dr Humburger was in turn liaising with the last remaining ex-

Mafia bishop, Il Ciprioni, to coordinate all the ex-Mafia family of assassins.

"Damn it," thought Sir Henry. "There are no other options to save the bank." He'd been rushed into sanctioning the ill-conceived Oxford contract 12 years ago. Damn it all. Damn, damn, damn. He was sure he could bring it all together now. He'd found out that the NYPB had a 25 per cent stake in the de Lafitte's nuclear research company, and that the de Lafitte family had freely donated another 25 per cent to the Vatican bank, now controlled by Il Ciprioni.

"To hell with charity, he thought. "Once the de Lafitte family is assassinated we'll get rid of Ciprioni too. Then I'll get full control of *Aligoté Nucléaire SA*. It's the only way to save the NYPB bank with billions to spare. The patent and licence fees alone will bring in millions of dollars annually."

Dr Humburger had spilled the beans by referring to the $1.5 billion cash balance that *Aligoté* had as reserves in their Swiss foundation in Geneva. This was key inside information of the private nuclear research and development company *Aligoté Nucléaire SA* – controlled through the de Lafitte Foundation – which did not have to publish accounts.

Sir Henry knew the worthlessness of all the platitudes he regularly trotted out to explain why his bank had never shone. "Really just a holding company, you know," he would say, varnishing the lies with various news-related excuses. "The exchange rate crisis, the collapse of Lloyd's, the Russian crisis, the Asian stock market collapse, September 11, the Iraq war, the 2008 crash with the consequent folding of major worldwide banks, etc.,etc.."

On and on the excuses issued forth, papering over the gaping cracks in the bank's financial structure. But unless this weekend's de Lafitte Protocol was achieved, it would be close to being all over. He recalled Mac's impertinence only last week, "Some of the boys think you're holding out on us, Harry," he'd said. He could've killed the bastard there and then, but had merely smiled graciously. "All will be revealed in the course of time ... so be patient, Mac."

Sir Henry shifted the right-hand side of his moustache just a fraction into a sneer, thinking, "Today Mac has indeed received his final answer." Sir Henry the ex-MI6 killer then stepped over the corpse casually, as if he'd just swatted a fly. But he did not notice the terrified eyes of the janitor, who had witnessed it all – and who was now retreating quietly into the broom cupboard, an extension of the boiler room. The poor fellow had been dismissed from his post earlier that same day by Mac and had taken refuge there to avoid going home after his shift had ended, not daring to announce the bad news to his poverty-stricken family.

Sir Henry reached the ground floor, opened the side door to the main entrance off the hall, and took a deep breath of freezing November air. The chauffeur jumped out of the long extended limousine which was to take him to Kennedy airport and, as he opened the wide side door, Sir Henry paused to make sure he had his air ticket to Kentucky. He pulled a wad of papers from his black velvet jacket pocket.

"What's this?" he thought. "The hunting fixtures list of the de Lafitte hounds? Aha." At dinner he'd been at pains to mention them. He'd said how, after many years of being pestered, he'd finally given in and become joint master of the Gordonston Hounds. He couldn't do anything but accept after being asked by his dearest friend personally – the former chairman of the bank, Senator Cecil Gordonston-Lafitte.

"Of course," Sir Henry had said at dinner, "Some day I knew I'd have to give in to him." Sir Henry blushed, ashamed of his dissembling and of his pains not to mention that he'd been wheedling for that very appointment for 15 years, ever since he'd come to the States. Nor did he allow himself even to think at that moment about how he had already worked out, in detail, the forthcoming murder of that same best friend.

As he stood beside the limousine the cold air cleared his mind. Today he should have been the happiest man in New York. Instead he was faced with the macabre fact that this fox-killing season would not only include the murder of his best friend but also all that friend's cousins, aunts and uncles, nieces and nephews – and all their senior relations throughout the world. Quite a Protocol indeed.

No amount of self-delusion or conjuring up of Chinese walls could prevent the contamination of his joy. Nor would it be easy to keep up his affable appearance at George Gordonston-Lafitte's hunt ball tonight. Daft idea, but of course typical of George. That ball always preceded the special lawn meet the next day known as George's Sunday. Already 24 hours were beginning to seem an age, with the anticipated slaughter of that large extended family.

Sir Henry, despite everything, had grown to love that family. He twitched as he realised that the European killings had already begun. As a reliable and experienced MI6 killer he had opted to undertake the murder of his best friend tomorrow evening, just as he always insisted on putting down all his favourite hunters himself. He had it all worked out already: it had been gone over so many times, and it relied entirely on Cecil Gordonston-Lafitte's unending goodwill. He'd lure Cecil to the top of the rickety library steps ... Cecil had always been such an obliging fellow. Yes, Cecil would certainly make the effort of fetching that book for us ... for me.

Sir Henry sighed. Thinking in the royal we was his customary habit of putting a desirable distance between himself and his murderous intentions. But it eluded him just now. Finally Sir Henry bent down, brushing away the snowflakes from the white leather upholstery of the limousine. He lowered himself in, about to reach for the drinks cabinet, but hesitated. "Should we fool ourselves into believing that we can now afford to get really drunk, to somehow wash away the heaviness of our murderous thoughts?" As the chauffeur closed the limousine door Sir Henry pulled open the small veneered walnut cabinet that was set into the back lining of the chauffeur's bench seat. The sparkling lights from the mirrored interior of the miniature bar dazzled him, as did the richer sparkling from the hand-cut Waterford Crystal whisky tumblers. "We can't go through with it without getting drunk – really drunk indeed," he said to himself.

With that thought he splashed some Glenfiddich single malt Scotch whisky into a crystal tumbler and closed his eyes, squeezing them tightly shut – drinking deeply and rapidly. Then he opened his eyes and spotted a brandy stain near the bottom button of his white waistcoat. He leaned forward, picked up some salt from an array of nuts in the small crystal dish standing beside the whisky bottle, and dropped a liberal dose of absorbent salt on to the brandy spot.

Sir Henry's thoughts now turned towards his father, who would have left him with huge debts but for the secret the old man had disclosed on his deathbed. That was the key that we needed. The old devil had forever kept everything wrapped up within himself. No doubt the information would have gone with him to his grave, but that night – for the first time he could remember – he'd shown some spontaneous affection for his old man.

It was the very night the Berlin Wall came down when Sir Henry had stayed up with his father, turning down the TV's volume and hearing the dying man's slobbering breathing. At the very last moment the old man, in a fit of whimpering hysteria, blurted it out. "Within the New York bank's vaults … hidden underneath mountains of pink papers … there's a dark green metal container … It contains … a share certificate … in the Swiss research company … *Aligoté Nucléaire SA*. It'll all be yours now, Harry … See Doctor … Hum … Hum … bur …"

But he'd never finished that last sentence. After years of searching Sir Henry finally located that rusty green box. It then took more years to track down the doctor. At the end of the hunt it wasn't difficult to persuade the lawyer to do a deal once Sir Henry had realised he was not a medical doctor but a lawyer – indeed, a Swiss trustee lawyer and the confidant of the de Lafitte family ($1 million in promissory notes had seen to that). What was less acceptable was the lawyer's further demand of a 10 per cent share of the total proceeds, without even the mere mention or suggestion of the many risky assassinations involved.

"But we'll take care of that greedy bastard in our own unique way," Sir Henry thought. Over the years Sir Henry had gleaned enough information from Humburger to understand the pre-eminent value of *Aligoté Nucléaire SA* within the nuclear industry – and, therefore, the significance of the NYPB's 25 per cent holding (and the peculiar equivalent holding of 25 per cent donated by the de Lafittes to the Vatican bank all those years ago). He'd suspected way back that there were many unanswered questions about the old man's bank. How, otherwise, had it continued in existence for all those years? And what deceptions lay beneath the sense of urgency, even desperation, in the old man's dying words? Neither father nor son was religious.

Funny thing, that. His great-great-grandparents, the ones who'd started as Quakers with the de Lafittes, had been so religious. On his deathbed his father must have been as close to a confession as he was capable of, except – even in the face of death – he'd not told him the full truth.

Sir Henry refilled his tumbler, splashing the pale Glenfiddich around the remaining ice cubes and – as he drank – he pictured himself snatching away the library steps from underneath Cecil, his dearest friend, and could hear quite clearly the crack of poor Cecil's neck snapping on the highly-polished wooden floor of the finest library in Kentucky. Sir Henry opened his eyes, feeling the white soft leather of the extended Cadillac envelope his body as the limousine sped off. "I have to relax my tired brain before meeting the senator for the last time in Kentucky," he thought. He drank deeply again, thinking, "Oh, to hell with it." He wasn't born yesterday, either.

Chapter Eight

Charles's alarm clock went off at 5 a.m.. A strange illumination highlighted the pale blue stripes of his bedroom. He instinctively swivelled his shoulders sideways, ready to jump out of bed, but the dead weight of his legs reminded him once more of the purpose of the bar overhead – which he now reached out for with his strong rowing hands and arms. He lifted up his body in line with the accumulated snow outside the Georgian window. The muscles of his naked arms quivered as, looking through the window, he maintained his position.

Then his eyes focused on the brightly-plumed Mandarin duck he'd saved last spring – the sole survivor out of a brood of six. This living jewel was strutting about in the snow, circling a solitary oak tree. Then it preened itself. Charles smiled as he remembered saving this one by swaddling it in one of his old cashmere pullovers. It and its siblings had lost their oil feathers, but Emperor had somehow regained them, the brave fellow.

Charles finally lowered his body down again and started to secure a body brace around his torso, then the aluminium calipers around his idle legs. But as he reached for his hunting kit he recalled Uncle Jacques's telephone call of last night, and frowned. His father had turned as white as a sheet before handing him the receiver – and Uncle Jacques's voice, usually vibrant and full of energy, seemed transformed into a careful, precise, calculated whisper. Was it not strange that after 12 years of intensive research (conducted by the world's best investigators) not a single hard fact had been unearthed until last night, just before another lawn meet?

Since the shooting Charles had decided to do all he could to get fitter and more agile in spite of his injuries, so that he might function independently again and do something positive with his life. The rowing squad at Oriel, having learned he'd survived the shooting, never let up encouraging him – especially when they'd heard the prognosis that he'd be on his back for the rest of his life.

He'd tried to listen to the doctor's verdict calmly, but refused to accept it as a given. What he did accept was that he'd have to learn everything from scratch, and he prayed that he'd always have the presence of mind to allow others to help him. But what Charles hadn't foreseen was the love and sheer determination of his father: this, and the stimulus he'd continued to receive from friends as the months and years wore on. It made him discover that the difficult part would always be the readiness to accept graciously any proffered help.

As Charles wound the long silk webbing of his hunting stock around his neck he tried to weigh up the significance of last night's phone call again. It was another 10 minutes before he finally had his stock in place, held with a plain gold pin. But by then he knew exactly what he was going to propose at his uncle's hunt breakfast later that morning.

Hearing his father's alarm clock go off across the landing he deftly placed an old-fashioned pair of wooden crutches under his armpits, reached down to click both latches of the calipers near his knees and swung effortlessly across the threshold to the landing. It was all second nature to him now. Spotting the familiar yellow strip of light under his father's door, he knocked before entering.

"Come," said a deep but kind voice. A whiff of 4711 Eau de Cologne still hung in the air as he kissed his father. "November snow, Charles?" chimed Sir Basil, as he peered fondly at the well-worn hunting kit of his own days as master of fox hounds that was still being put to good use by his 39-year-old son. Charles chuckled as he swung himself through the bottle green bedroom towards the tall red shutters, and prised open the black security latches with a loud clatter.

"And some." Charles gestured outside the window. "If it's like this outside Paris, might not Uncle Jacques have to cancel his stag hunt?"

"Goodness, no," Sir Basil said excitedly, rocking on his four-poster bed before stretching himself to look out at the thick snow on the windowsill.

"With solidly frozen turf, yes – to save the horses their joints and the hounds their pads. But it'll take more than one snowfall for my brother to call off his lawn meet." In old age Sir Basil seemed keener than ever. "Jacques will release a boxed stag first, then he'll switch to the strong outlier who escaped last season. There'll be sport for you today, Charles." The old man rubbed his hands together slowly with a big grin on his face, looking up with pride at his son – who was propped up against one of the pillars of the huge four-poster.

"Yes, I'm looking forward to it," Charles grinned. "Oh, did you hear? George wants me to fly over for his Kentucky do tonight. I did think I might go, as I'll be able to test our new jet on my way there."

"Good idea, Charles. I should. And I'd stay on for his mad lawn meet, too. Sunday, isn't it?" The old man didn't try to hide his excitement. They looked at each other fondly, before Charles threw back his head, chuckling.

"Cousin George is always fun, isn't he?" Both of them had long overcome the presence of Charles's disability as an obstacle to anything, viewing it now merely as a reminder of retaining a positive outlook for the daily adventures of life on God's earth. Sir Basil did notice Charles's specially-widened white breeches inside his enlarged black leather hunting boots (they camouflaged his aluminium calipers), but he said nothing.

"Anything I can do for you before I leave?" The young man's grace touched his father, who shook his head slowly from side to side. Then he hesitated, contradicting himself. "Charles … yes.", "It'll cause so much unhappiness … I mean within." Sir Basil drummed his chest. "Yes. Try and talk your sister Anne out of her intended divorce. Impress upon her what she must already know."

A dark look clouded his face. "Above all, remind her that it is a mortal sin." He rested his head on his bed cushion, changing the subject."

"Assassination." He again mouthed the word very slowly, "Ass … ass … in … a … tion. Jacques never used that word before, other than to dismiss it. It's the first time he's ever taken it seriously." Sir Basil's concerned eyes were on his son's face but Charles was already looking down, trying to adjust the calipers inside his hunting boots. He replied in a light-hearted manner.

"The French *Sécurité* have insisted on hunting with us this morning. They always talk about how efficient they are." Once more he kissed his father, who slipped him a battered old faded pink envelope with the words, "I've wanted to give this to you so many times, Charles. It's your mama's beautiful poem, which she sent me three years before we were married. Share it with your distant cousin Dr Caroline next time you see her. She's very fond of it too. Did I not tell you that I discussed it with her last year?

Charles sensed the envelope contained something very special. Entranced, he removed its contents and looked at the poem:

True Love
Love, if it be true, is pure and full of grace
Then discipline when fighting adversity
Defending that precious love is never waste
As it is bound to transform love to ecstasy.
Love is never confined by time or places:
They are mere allusions to its constancy.
Since love is timeless, years are but mere seconds.
Love's greatest gift? Indeed, it is self-giving.
Love is prudent, is just, brave and temperate.
It is forever growing and always living,
Gently burning, 'though it is never timid.
God's love for us is the best proof of himself.
Pray that our love for him be the proof of ourselves.

Charles smiled, his eyes glistening with tears of joy. He was thrilled to read his mother's insights and marvelled at her open calligraphy. As he reinserted the poem carefully back into its envelope he kissed it and then slipped it into his breast pocket. "You always told me that Mama was an angel. I shall look forward to reading it at my leisure soon." His eyes brimmed over with tears of joy as he looked up again, and went back to his father's earlier concern.

"Don't worry, Pappa. I'll be discussing the security with Uncle Jacques in the greatest of detail." Halfway out of the door Charles turned around, with an I've-forgotten-something look on his face. "Today's St Andrew's day – the last Saturday of November. I promised young Rupert I'd bring him to his first wall game. Oh well, it can't be helped. Do apologise to him on my behalf."

The old man raised his hand. "Don't worry. I'll take him myself. That's if he's really better. Tell Anne I'll explain Parham's rules to him. Tell my brother to be careful – and you too, my boy."

"Bye-bye, Papa. Give Rupert my love, too," Charles said lightly. "It'll only take me 15 minutes to get to Oxford Airport and then less than an hour to the chateau in our new jet." After Charles had swung himself out of the room the old man sat upright in bed and blessed himself. "I'm proud of you, my boy. God be with you." Basil Russell-Lafitte continued:

"In the name of the Father, the Son, and the Holy Spirit, Amen. Good morning, dear Jesus. I give you this day my body, my soul, my work and my play. Our Father, who art in Heaven, hallowed be thy name. Thy kingdom come. Thy will be done on earth as it is in Heaven. Give us this day our daily bread, and forgive us our trespasses as we forgive those who trespass against us. And lead us not into temptation, but deliver us from evil. Amen."

So Sir Basil, like most of his close friends in his circle, began his daily morning prayers – and his were offered for the safe return of his son, the "brave fellow."

Chapter Nine

"Damn that snow." Il Perfetto, the mature ex-Mafia assassin, cursed bitterly in his peasant Italian on his arrival before dawn that Saturday at Paris's Charles de Gaulle airport. Yet, while he fumed at the unexpected snow, it did not appear to him to be especially cold in Paris.

There was a dark anger on his face as he disembarked before dawn. The professional assassin had not made any allowance for snow, of all the eventualities. "Damn, damn, damn," he cursed inwardly.

Two hours later – once inside the 30,000 acres of the Lafitte forest – he listened suspiciously to the barely-audible crunching of his footsteps in the unscheduled November snow, thinking, "------- sticky snow, too. Damn well clings to my shoes with every step I take." The leather of his light brown Italian shoes was already dark, sodden with moisture. White frozen flakes covered the dead leaves underneath the ancient beech trees – whose moss-furred roots, covered with endless white flakes, stretched out like massive whitewashed elephant trunks.

His heart jumped at the lone, eerie cry of a de Lafitte staghound awakening in the kennels some distance from the chateau. Il Perfetto turned his permanently-tanned face in that direction as more hounds joined in, their hollow lamenting notes filling him with unease. Nonetheless, he forced himself to move stealthily among the bare trees until he'd reached the edge of the clearing. Looking up at a rare tall evergreen Canadian cedar tree he thought about his younger brother, the eldest of the Tre Terzina triplets.

Poor bastard. He tried to imagine how young Il Terzina must have felt 12 years ago, straddled up one of those massive branches. The poor fellow's mobile must have scared him shitless when it vibrated against his cold skin, 12 years ago – minutes after the Oxford assassination failure, when desperate attempts had been made by the ex-Mafia don to call off the whole operation.

The knock-on effect had been near chaos. But the ex-don's luck had held – except for the cable car murder in China, involving the inventor at *Aligoté Nucléaire SA*, Dr Guy de Lafitte and his wife. Only one positive thing had been achieved, as far as the ex-don was concerned: his luck had held out, concealing al-Qaeda's botched butchery for 12 years. Through the application of brute force the ex-don insisted on the absolute adherence to old-fashioned *omertà*. That had indeed secured total silence.

Il Perfetto shuddered at the thought of it. It was entirely their own fault. How typical of the family to be making demands on him now. It was blackmail. "But then," he thought, "I should have realised that they would never have allowed me to escape scot-free."

The ex-Mafia don should have known all along why he, as his eldest son, couldn't get involved. The ex-don had taken advantage of the intimate secret he'd been given about Il Ragazzo, Il Perfetto's estranged son. Apart from the fact that he should have known that the preparation and planning would never be up to be up to the high, exacting standards of Il Perfetto the ex-don should have known in his heart that the eldest remaining son had been right to refuse to take part. But he never suspected the ex-don would go so far as to divulge his secret.

Il Perfetto closed his watery eyes tight and stood shivering in the morning air, thinking deeply. He still felt that baffled, protective, indelible fatherly love towards Il Ragazzo, that baby he'd kidnapped in Oxford, just as he'd felt it 39 years ago when an Oxford midwife had handed him his unconscious wife's stillborn baby. No sooner had she handed him over to him than the midwife had wanted the baby back, with her eyes clearly focused on a disposable bin.

"After all those years of yearning, our very own baby," Il Perfetto thought. The baby was blue in death, still covered in the off-white cloudy wax of childbirth and his wife was in a coma. He'd snarled at the midwife, who'd fled in terror, then he'd bolted from that room hugging the tiny corpse. Il Perfetto could still remember feeling like a wild animal when he'd stormed down the endless corridors of Oxford's maternity ward.

Eventually he'd found himself alone inside an empty suite marked PRIVATE in large capitals. The room was bare except for two transparent plastic cots, in which two near-identical twin babies were asleep. Through the half-open door of an adjoining room he heard the stifled sobs of a man moaning in grief. In a flash he scooped up one of the twins, leaving his own dead baby in its place.

But at the very moment of leaving that room he'd sensed there was something wrong. He'd made a mistake. The live baby had a tiny plastic armband around its wrist. His stillborn's wrist was bare. He'd realised it just in time. He could still remember boiling with anger because the midwife hadn't even placed one on his stillborn baby's wrist.

Il Perfetto retraced his steps then bent over and removed the baby corpse again, placing it on nearby weighing scales. Then he put the live twin back into its own transparent plastic cot. With the forefinger of each of his hands inside the thin plastic of the armband he pulled gently, stretching it – slipping it off the live twin's wrist while it started to cry. Quickly, he switched the armband on to the wrist of his own lifeless baby before replacing it in the cot.

Both live babies were now bawling as Il Perfetto rushed from that room with one of the crying twins cradled beneath the black folds of his scarf. The next thing he remembered was – as she'd regained consciousness – placing the stolen baby with its peculiar high forehead to suckle at his wife's breast. A wondrous look of joy had replaced her earlier sad frown. It took Il Perfetto but a few seconds to scoop up his wife – who was suckling the baby in the white hospital linen of the bed – and place both wife and baby on to a nearby wheelchair. He rolled them out of the hospital and, without further ado, bundled them into his hired car.

Over the years the child revealed his inbred intelligence. Il Perfetto never told his wife about the switch, and always joined her in praising their gifted boy. Il Ragazzo was their natural name for the child. Seven years later, when his wife was dying, he whispered her a hint of the truth. She'd smiled sweetly, as if she'd suspected something all the time, and then she asked to see Il Ragazzo alone for a few minutes. Had she told him? Surely not. But Il Perfetto never saw his son alone after that.

Access to his boy thereafter had become formal: everything had to be through Il Perfetto's own father, the ex-don, on his knees. Always begging on his knees. The boy had grown up in Italy, in Palermo, and later he had been spirited off to the USA.

Desperately lonely, Il Perfetto knew immediately he'd made a serious mistake when he telephoned the ex-don's bastard son, Il Ciprioni – who by then had contrived his appointment as the last remaining ex-Mafia bishop. That bastard was already plotting to become a cardinal. Il Ciprioni had scoffed at Il Perfetto's plea for help.

"Never contact me again," he'd hissed. "Is that clear? Never again." Then, in 2004, five years after the Oxford fiasco, there was nothing else inside the envelope Il Perfetto had received that day again on the last Saturday of November … just one coloured photo of his boy, Il Ragazzo, with his high forehead. He was now grown up, tall, good-looking and shaking hands with a cleric. The photograph had obviously been professionally taken through a long lens.

The cleric wore a scarlet patch underneath his dog collar – was he a bishop or something? The photograph showed two men talking in front of the United Nations building in New York. On the reverse in a thick black scrawl were these words: "Me, talking to your son, Il Ragazzo. Your estranged son." Il Perfetto could just make out the pink postmark – *Roma* – on the large envelope. It was barely visible on a small yellow Italian stamp.

There and then Il Perfetto realised again that resisting the family was a no-go area. The creep who'd sent that photo was telling him loud and clear that he now knew his secret. He knew about Il Ragazzo – his son, his boy.

Il Perfetto squirmed as it'd dawned on him that the bishop in the photo could be none other than the ex-don's bastard son Il Ciprioni, his own half-brother. Il Perfetto had always assumed he would be able to keep his secret strictly between himself and his father after he had confided his secret to him on his knees, as in a confessional. That too had become another dream gone wrong. So that photo and the secret it symbolised had been the tool of coercion used to enlist Il Perfetto's matchless skills as an assassin. What was it about this Oxford contract? Why had it not been totally abandoned after that disaster 12 years ago?

Il Perfetto knew he was wrong to have assumed that they'd give the Oxford contract a new name and then ask him to execute it. He remembered so clearly that thought flashing through his mind as he pocketed the photo at the time. The bastards. It had taken him five years to prepare for today's assassinations.

Then two years ago Il Perfetto's father summoned him to Campione, the Italian tax haven, the tiny enclave on the lake of Lugano near the Swiss and Italian borders. A secret no-man's-land, with its own peculiar tax laws: still in Italy but accessible only from Switzerland. He knew that he'd not been invited to gamble in the local casino. Il Perfetto forced himself to re-examine everything in detail every day. "That is why I've never failed," he thought.

His father the ex-don had safely holed himself up in self-imposed exile in a simple goat farmer's cottage in Campione. Il Perfetto and his father had embraced on meeting that afternoon. All seemed forgiven and they'd hugged each other warmly. After a lot of catching-up talk the old man went for his usual pre-dinner rest in anticipation of the massive meal being prepared by the ex-don's deaf retainer.

The feast had really been terrific, like the old days, but as the last pangs of hunger were satisfied the father's and the son's respective demands began to be repeated. Then –as always after a few hours – they began to interrupt each other. Heated arguments became interspersed with brief attempts at a truce, which in the past consisted in retiring to another room – in this case to a chocolate-coloured brown one, a sitting room-cum-cluttered study – before losing all control.

Their bawling was only overwhelmed by the non-stop playing of the *Three Tenors* album at maximum volume, so as not to alarm the neighbouring farmers or the filthy rich tax-evaders in their spacious adjoining villas. On and on it went into the small hours, with full wine glasses in their hands – then back into the kitchen for the next course, before reverting back again to the leather armchairs of the ex-don's den. With no solution in sight they eventually rolled, cursing, into their beds.

Next morning they had embraced each other with renewed respect before sitting down in the bright sunlight of the veranda, which was perfumed with freshly-roasted Italian coffee and fresh bread. Sleep had allowed the ninety-year-old ex-Mafia don to weigh up his age and experience against Il Perfetto's cunning but heartfelt convictions.

Abruptly, during breakfast, Il Perfetto's as-yet-unshaven father (with his white stubble) had withdrawn to take a telephone call in his bedroom. After half an hour he came back properly shaven into the sunlight, embraced his son once more and invited him once again into his den. There, the ex-don gestured to Il Perfetto to take one of the plastic armchairs. The don himself sat down in his own larger black one, made of thick black leather.

With both his elbows resting lightly on the edge of the armrests the ex-don carefully brought the tips of his crooked fingers together before parting his cupped hands again – and gestured smoothly towards Il Perfetto in a conciliatory manner that was matched by a glint of light in his dark eyes.

"I am now asking you, my eldest surviving son, to set out once more – very slowly – your final thoughts, to a father who has always respected you. Yes? … True." The ex-Mafia don had answered his own rhetorical question himself grimly, with a dark smirk slightly parting his lips. He readjusted his elbows again on top of the armrests and moved his crooked fingers together again before closing his eyes.

He'd listened with full concentration and in total silence for more than an hour to Il Perfetto's plans then lowered his head until his top lip touched both of his forefingers, one of which was his trigger finger. But he still continued listening. After a further hour he started to lean forward, still with his elbows on the black armrests, and began sucking both his index fingers. He'd remained totally calm throughout, concentrating as he listened, until the tone of Il Perfetto's voice finally changed. Hard reason had slowly altered to a barely perceptible plea for understanding.

That was when the ex-don also removed his fingers from his lips and slowly opened his arms in a wide circular open gesture, turning his palms upwards in a forgiving gesture with a soft understanding moan – and had simply and sweetly said, "Agreed."

Without changing his posture the ex-don very slowly gestured with the tops of his ill-shaped fingers towards Il Perfetto to come to him. As Il Perfetto buckled his knee and knelt down in front of the ex-don. The old man placed the fingers of each hand on Il Perfetto's cheeks, leaned forward and kissed the crown of Il Perfetto's bare skin. He always did this when he was undertaking a vow. It was the ex-don's personal stamp of approval and Il Perfetto, his eldest son, kissed the old man's hand formally in return.

Il Perfetto thought, with a knowing smile, "God help any poor bastard who'd try and come between us now." This display of bonding was the precursor to the drama of the battleground that would involve all of the assassin's family for the foreseeable future.

Il Perfetto and his father now began to talk quietly, in the easy, friendly, soothing tones of yesteryear's conspiracies. Large sums of money would be involved and, with it, tight control at the top – which the old man knew matched Il Perfetto's own ideas of tight accountability. The ex-Mafia don now saw why Il Perfetto needed direct control in Europe. He saw also why he needed worldwide control.

They would still use Sir Henry Steere's old slogan for the project – The de Lafitte Protocol – but otherwise all of Il Perfetto's earlier conditions, including the absence of Osama bin Laden's al-Qaeda involvement, were confirmed as a matter of course. Also … his son Il Ragazzo's involvement would be strictly limited to the USA. The ex-Mafia don knew that Il Ragazzo, like his father Il Perfetto, had never failed to complete a contract.

The old man had wisely insisted – many years ago, after the Oxford fiasco – that Il Ragazzo should withdraw completely until he was called for. Il Perfetto always wondered where the old man got his foresight from, and he then knew that it came from worrying - constantly, ceaselessly - and age-old experience. It was therefore agreed that it'd be up to the ex-don to get Il Ragazzo back into harness to complete this final one-off assignment.

Il Perfetto readily conceded that Il Ragazzo's twin, Charles Russell-Lafitte, could now be taken out after all in Europe. He even agreed that one of the Tre Terzina triplets should try again but the ex-don insisted on doing it himself, and nothing would change his mind. "It is for me my last honour killing now," he said.

Over a light lunch Il Perfetto had outlined exactly what needed to be done, how it should be done … and the right time to do it. He saw that the old man was pleased. He was glad that his father was proud of him, but he also insisted that everyone else in the family should rally and shape up. He spelled it out clearly once more.

"They'll all ------- well need to start an immediate and rigid daily exercise routine. It will only be allowed to come to an end when I say so, and the end of the job will be indicated only when the $5 million fee is -------- well banked. It is all subject to one final proviso - under no circumstances would the involvement of al-Qaeda be allowed to ruin our affairs again."

"Bravo," the ex-don had chimed in as his son ended his demands. It was also understood that the ex-Mafia don would ensure that Il Ragazzo would be removed from Osama bin Laden's personal influence, if any.

Il Perfetto was happy, except for the fact that Bishop Ciprioni was still involved. The ex-don's bastard son would always remain a bastard and Il Perfetto knew he'd never be able to trust him. "Not that I'd ever done so before," Il Perfetto remembered thinking, and spat out those words. The ex-don had smiled awkwardly but nodded, with this exclamation and accompanying shrug: "Bastards can't stop themselves from being bastards."

* * *

Il Perfetto had recalled all this as he stood in the snow of the de Lafitte family forest. Now he swung down his untidy traditional fishing pouch – which had been weighing heavily on his right shoulder – and carefully placed its broad-bottomed end, which contained the sniper rifle, on to the snow. Painfully, he straightened his back.

Chapter Ten

The stippled haze of the Parisian lights was visible through snow clouds as Fred the pilot handed the controls of the latest de Lafitte supersonic jet to Charles.

"Here goes," Charles called out as he cranked up the power and rammed the polished aluminium steering column forward, gulping for air when he felt his stomach in his throat. He held the vertical dive, feeling the adrenalin surge through his body as he hurtled down through layer upon layer of blinding snow with his eyes locked, laser-like, on a bank of instruments. "Isn't this exciting?" he called out, unaware of Fred's blanched, speechless face beside him.

Charles smoothly pulled out of the vertical dive into a softly spiralling arc, scattering a broad swathe of snow from the treetops of his uncle's avenue. "Shall we do that again?" he laughed.

Before Fred could find his voice Charles launched the jet into another large loop, skimming low over the bare elms of the avenue and whipping up snow into a blinding mist. Then, without commentary, he sent the jet up into a vertical ascent in front of the top windows of the chateau. After another loop he finally landed the eight-seater aircraft vertically, next to the helicopters parked beside the formal tennis courts.

Charles brushed back his mop of hair from his high forehead. "Don't worry. I'll take all the blame for waking everybody up." With that he sought his wooden crutches. "Take the day off and see Paris, Fred. We'll meet tonight at Orly airport before heading for Kentucky at 20.00 hours. Then we'll really be able to put this baby through its paces." The pilot didn't say anything, but marvelled at the young man's energy.

Charles grabbed his wooden crutches and opened the aircraft's door and – with the help of an overhead pulley – lowered himself down on the virgin snow in one smooth movement. He clicked his leg braces and swung himself briskly through the thick snow past the tennis courts on the left, swinging on his crutches like a pendulum towards the chateau.

Refreshed by the cold air filling his lungs, he thought of his uncle – whom he knew would want to talk about the death threats and the dangers to the de Lafitte foundation due to them not having a family successor. There would probably be some sinister stuff about the Chinese Nuclear Acquisitions Peace (so-called) Programme (CNAPP) as well.

His uncle had often hinted at CNAPP's surreptitious infiltration of bona fide nuclear research programmes – and this theme would doubtless be taken up again today between steam room sessions, a formal tasting of the chateau's maturing wines and that evening's elaborate dinner, making this year's breakfast meeting at the chateau all the more significant.

Charles hadn't hunted for 12 years, apart from his recent cubbing sessions with the Kildare hounds. He felt somewhat apprehensive - but felt very close to Uncle Jacques, especially as his field master on the hunting field ... and he now wanted to do that again – and deal with the Foundation, if he could. Yet he was in two minds as to his life's journey. Should he allow himself to be persuaded to abandon the postgraduate degree in theology he was only just beginning, or decide to become Uncle Jacques's full-time understudy immediately?

There was no doubt as to the mind of the family. After all, that was why he had taken his doctorate in nuclear energy 12 years ago. His new degree at Oxford was already under way, he had already dealt with the long reading list and he'd long overcome his aversion to swapping inane jokes with pimply freshmen again. But did he really feel comfortable reading for another degree? He imagined the coming exhortation from Uncle Jacques, pronounced in an *Ancien Régime* French that was smooth, urbane and swarming with characteristically labyrinthine subjunctives.

"You might not know it, Charles, but I think I can say that I have been broadly authorised by all the families to speak to you. It would seem that they might feel very much happier – and you might feel more effectively challenged – if you were to decide to undertake my *stage* (Jacques always made full use of that superlative French word for training) sooner rather than later ... thereby not only safeguarding the future of our massive family investments in Geneva but also ensuring the future of the nuclear energy industry for France. Perhaps (even more rewardingly) you could help keep the balance of power by helping to monitor and prevent the reckless spread of nuclear armaments."

Charles was hopeful that this breakfast meeting would at the very least clarify all the options – and that his own proposal of appointing a professional manager would eventually find approval – as it would take the focus away from Jacques, thereby safeguarding his life too. As Charles's boots crunched on the snow-covered gravel his solemn features broke into a warm grin as he caught the smell of freshly-ground coffee and hot French croissants wafting up from the chateau's basement fans. He looked up at the icy limestone steps, placed the left wooden crutch underneath the thumb of his right hand and grabbed the metal icy railings with his free left hand. Swinging one leg up at a time he hauled his body up, repeating the laborious procedure until he reached the terrace ... and finally straightened himself, an iced sheen of perspiration on his brow.

Before moving between the pillars of the chateau he turned around, admiring the snow-covered spacious lawns and the two stretches of lakes with their thin layers of ice and snow. He was reminded of the confidence displayed by his French ancestors. Where was the frenzied madness spoken of by left-wing modern cynics in creating such beauty? With that, the title of a book sprang to mind: *The Beauty of Holiness and the Holiness of Beauty: Art, Sanctity and the Truth of Catholicism* by the Oxford author, Fr. John Saward.

The Cavalier King Charles spaniel and the multitude of Yorkshire terriers that had started to bark inside the chateau now lurched forward as Uncle Jacques himself opened the front door. The Irish wolfhound Guinness, who lay in front of the blazing fire in the hall, merely swivelled his eyes towards the commotion: he was disinclined to move away from the warmth passing through the club fender.

"Charles."

"Uncle Jacques."

They exchanged three kisses, at once inclusive and exclusive.

"Come inside, Charles. My French cook has prepared us a full English breakfast in your honour." As they entered the dining room eight French men, attired in dark blue Sécurité jodhpurs, rose from their chairs. For a second all eyes were on Charles's wooden crutches — but were soon inevitably redirected to Charles's infectious smile, and they began smiling themselves.

Charles listened attentively as breakfast progressed, but he remained silent. He'd heard it all before: the annual ritual had become second nature to him. But what was Uncle Jacques holding back, and why?

Chapter Eleven

Il Perfetto heard the supersonic bang as the overhead jet went through the sound barrier, followed by a loud, thundering roar through the Lafitte forest that morning.

Instinctively the assassin dived for protection among the large snow-covered roots of the nearby ancient beech trees, even though the ear-piercing blast vanished in an instant. Moments later the low-flying jet came somersaulting back again – even lower this time, blasting through the icy wind and hurling snow from the treetops of the avenue in a fine mist.

Il Perfetto wedged himself down deeper among the snow-covered leaves and covered his ears, afraid the sound would damage his ageing eardrums. Bewildered, the assassin cowered motionless and stayed there at the edge of the wood's main clearing. He regretted the years of brittle disagreement with his father. "Hopefully it'd be all over for good, with a successful outcome after this weekend," he thought. As the sound died down his thoughts turned to the reasons for his mission today, and he reminded himself that he had never failed.

With his senses still raw, he looked up through the haze of the snow mist. Squinting through the swirling flakes, his eyes settled on the endless rows of leaning wooden stakes in the forest clearing. The snow-clad rows of commercial timber poles resembled one giant igloo settlement. There was a worried expression on his suntanned features when he kept on looking around, as though he'd lost his bearings. "Bloody hell," he cursed in frustration ... but, collecting himself, he started counting each snow-covered mound with his right trigger finger, swearing in peasant Italian as he lost his count again.

He started again, carefully this time, from the furthest igloos – which were only tiny specks not far from a marsh-like pond where he knew the hunted stags invariably sought refuge.

Eventually his face twitched as he recognised the snow-covered bracken against one of the larger stacks of wooden poles some distance away in the main clearing in front of him. He checked his luminous watch, calculating how long it would take him to cross the snowbound open space.

Time was running out. In a few hours, he estimated, it would be bright – and the whole forest would shake with the drumming of thundering hoofs, horn music and the scary noise of those fiery staghounds. He pursed his lips, his face pulsating with determination as he cradled the long, heavy fishing pouch in both his arms. He was preparing himself and ready to run.

But he'd heard another strange sound, or was it the hostile wind? And again he rooted himself to the ground – silent, waiting – wanting to be sure. He thought, "There'll be several unknown bastards involved at the top now, plotting and scheming."

He knew one of those bastards, for sure. It was the sender of the photo – his half-brother, the ex-don's bastard son Il Ciprioni, whose very existence he wasn't even supposed to be aware of. Il Perfetto knew that ex-Mafia bishop only too well. He was the last remaining one of his type in the Vatican: a sly cunning man who wanted to become a cardinal no matter what the cost. He was a total danger zone. But as long as he and the other string-pullers at the top didn't interfere with his attention to detail this weekend he couldn't give a toss what they had in mind, as long as they didn't cramp his style. One clean shot today will take care of the acting head of that damn de Lafitte family.

He swallowed hard, thinking of the natural successor to the Comte Jacques: Charles Russell-Lafitte, whom he'd refused to murder 12 years ago once he'd finally realised the astonishing facts of his own kidnapped son's origins.

He worried again about his father, the ex-Mafia don. He loved that old man in spite of the fact that he had betrayed his secret. That his father could have allowed himself to be persuaded by that bastard Ciprioni to come out of retirement … What the bloody hell was that bastard thinking of? Il Perfetto knew that they were short-staffed, but he was also aware that his father was 89 … 90 years old.

The Parisian assassination tonight was theoretically very simple - it was a close-range hit – but, equally, the old man's sight was failing. What if he missed? His initial instinct had been to protest but, fearing another harrowing disagreement, he compromised again for the sake of peace in the family. The annihilation of the rest of the de Lafittes would take place in Europe and then America (which was Il Ragazzo's territory) proceeding to Ireland at Druid's Glen, then concluding in Panama or Auckland in New Zealand.

Another strange sound? He continued to listen. It was the wind, surely? He sprang into motion, pounding through the virgin snow, leaning forward with a loping, bearlike movement against the howling wind. The sharp gusts, which continued to lift up the powdery snow around him, whirled, whistled up and down and soared in the open clearing. But it didn't stop him becoming conscious of the snow caking unevenly on the soles of his Italian shoes. "I should have changed my shoes," he thought, but he well hadn't a chance before getting into the Ferrari he borrowed from an ex-Mafia colleague that morning.

He kept on running, pounding through the snow, trying to stop the heavy weapon hidden in the fishing tackle bag that was throwing him off balance. The twinge in his chest reminded him with alarm of his doctor's warning. But he couldn't afford to stop now even though the long, camouflaged weapon continued to lurch out of control, swinging heavily from left to right.

The hard lumps of frozen snow beneath his fine Italian shoes finally unbalanced him. Already winded, he smothered his cry through gritted teeth and braced his elbows in anticipation – aware that he must at all costs protect the deadly weapon hidden in the fishing pouch.

Bellyflopping in the snow, he prevented the fishing pouch hitting the ground with his elbows but worried that someone might have spotted him. As he scrambled in the snow he ignored the pain of his twisted ankle, and was already on his feet as he tried to recover his momentum. The pangs in his chest became unbearable but in spite of the excruciating torture he forced himself to run on. Another 50 strides … Bloody hell … He must make it … Damn it, he must keep on running … "This is gut-wrenching," he thought … another couple of steps … one more … at last. With that he dived down beside the snow-covered mound, letting out a suffocating scream through clenched teeth.

"Bloody hell," he panted feverishly, groaning like an animal through his teeth … he must stop himself from gasping loudly, uncontrollably. On all fours now, falling again, Il Perfetto rolled on his back squirming with pain – his hot breath was searing, burning his swelling gums. Aware of his weak heart, he turned on his side – and then over again on to the other side ... over and over until finally, on his belly, he just lay there slowly recovering ... panting ... wheezing.

Then – fully realising where he was – he started scratching, fumbling in the snow with more energy now, wildly ... He shoved occasional fistfuls of snow into his burning mouth. Then he stopped, sighing with relief, as he'd found what he was looking for. He started tugging furiously with it, like a famished wolf tearing apart a snow rabbit. The swirling wind whipped up the virgin snow again, and he was gone.

Chapter Twelve

That morning in Oxford the 87-year-old Sir Basil Russell-Lafitte lowered the worn clipboard on which he was writing his memoirs.

He looked up again through the Georgian windows of his bedroom, where the rising sun was slowly starting to disperse the November snow and mist. His imagination guided his eyes over the snow-covered lawns and trees and on into the distance, towards the ever-familiar spires of Oxford.

There his inner eye with a sharp memory opened the photo albums of his mind: the dome of the Radcliffe Camera, the spires of his old college and that of Magdalen College and the Tom Tower at Christ Church. He strolled through the libraries, the tutorials, the lecture rooms and the chapels, once more indulging in the delights of High Table - occasions of strange intrigues and measured excess.

It was among the hidden layers of these slumbering reflections that Sir Basil spent most of his days now. Suddenly there was a bustle of energy on top of him, breaking into Sir Basil's reverie: Sir Basil's daughter Anne's 13-year-old son bounded up on to his grandfather's four-poster bed, kissing the old man's stubbled cheeks.

"Good morning, Grandpa." Rupert's high-pitched soprano voice echoed around the bedroom. "Aha, Rupert," Sir Basil welcomed the boy. "It seems your pneumonia has finally disappeared. It has done a bunk, Rupert."

"Done a bunk, Grandpa?" the boy queried, as he tried to come to grips with this 19th-century expression in his distinctive French accent. "But guess what, Grandpa?" he quizzed the old man, with fresh-faced innocence. "Isn't it the wall game today?"

"Of course. It must be. Just let us double-check that again, Rupert." Sir Basil reached for the Eton fixtures list, which was propped against the brass lamp on his bedside table. His hand was still steady, though emaciated with age. His signet ring hung loosely around his left little finger. "Hmm. The feast day of St Andrew … yes. Here we are. Well done, Rupert." He smiled broadly at his grandson, who grinned proudly, asking, "Can you come too, Grandpa?"

The old man looked fondly at his daughter's clear blue eyes in the boy's face. "I don't think it will do us any real harm, do you?"

"I don't think so, Grandpa, and I'll be able to see my friends again before short leave. I wish Mama and Papa could've come." The boy added, solemnly, "Isn't Uncle Charles coming too?"

"Oh, Charles didn't want to wake you up this morning before he left for Paris. He's gone hunting with your Great Uncle Jacques." The old man planted a kiss on his grandson's forehead. "Charles'll be meeting up with your mama this evening in Paris, or even at the stag hunt itself. Isn't it exciting?"

The boy's eyes sparkled at the news. "Good," he said, giving his grandfather another peck on the cheek before he slid off the bed. "I'll just go and check if Webb has everything ready." Rupert bustled out through the bedroom door, ran along the gallery down the main staircase along the freezing stone-flagged hallway and out through the double front door. He kept running along the cleared snow passage down the granite steps in front of the house. Continuing without hesitating, he ran across the cleared snow that had covered the gravel before stepping on to the running board at the chauffeur's door of Sir Basil's ancient Phantom V Rolls-Royce.

"Isn't she a beauty, Webb?" Rupert stroked the blue polished bonnet as if the old motor was a puppy dog being minded by Webb.

Sir Basil's former army batman smiled dutifully, but continued with his task of warming up the engine. "Guess what, Webb?" Rupert thought of Webb as an indispensable friend of the family in whom he could confide. "Grandpa's bringing me to the wall game today."

"Very good, Master Rupert." Webb had been through it all so many times for many years before with Charles and all his friends. "Now, Master Rupert, if you get into the driving seat beside me here, I'll ask you to hold on to this knob just for three minutes. Then slowly push it in - very slowly, mind. It takes lots of patience to warm up this old engine. I've got to take the morning's post and *The Telegraph* upstairs."

* * *

"The letters and *The Telegraph*, sir," Webb said, as he entered Sir Basil's bedroom. He detected the smell of the fresh polish from his own black boots and allowed himself a small grin, but froze when he realised he'd forgotten to exchange his plain tweed for his smart chauffeur's cap. He swiftly removed the tweed as he thrust forward the bundle of papers. He cast his eyes about, checking whether his master's wooden shaving brush was still standing beside the teacup. No, he saw, it was floating in the open water jug beside the teacup, with a used throwaway razor lying on the saucer. This was his cue to remove the breakfast tray. He held it up high in front of his chest, checking whether his master had indeed shaved properly, and now waited the day's instructions.

* * *

Many years ago Sir Basil had been a law professor – and for many more years before that, as a junior don, he'd been a confirmed bachelor. Then to everyone's surprise, at the late age of 40, he had married one of the famous young Russell girl triplets.

With a large house to look after the young bride was delighted her husband had decided to retain the services of his batman, Webb – who was allocated the role of chauffeur, together with the more important role of general factotum. Webb had over many years become an indispensable necessity and friend of the whole family.

But Sir Basil's wife had died giving birth to twin boys two years after the birth of their first child, Anne. At the last moment the hospital's Catholic chaplain (who'd been called to her bedside) had sent urgently for her husband and his friend, Sir Basil, who was utterly distraught and confused with grief at her weak condition. She only lasted to complete the rosary and be given the last sacrament of Extreme Unction.

With the subsequent discovery of the apparent death of one of the twins Sir Basil had asked for the dead baby to be buried with his wife. There had been subdued whispers in the delivery room about two live babies, but rumours about one of the twins having suffered a cot death had also been circulating. All speculation was effectively quashed when Sir Bail's wishes became known about the funeral arrangements. A nurse was quietly reassigned from the maternity ward to fill another post and the file was permanently closed. There was never a question of Sir Basil ever remarrying.

* * *

"Thank you, Webb," Sir Basil said as Webb turned to go. "We'll be leaving shortly, and bringing young Rupert to the wall game."

"Very good, sir. I'll bring the heated blankets to the car, sir." With that he left the room. Sir Basil lifted up an unusual stiff envelope with a Swiss stamp. As he inserted his decorated silver paper knife he noticed the family lawyer's name, Dr Humburger, on the back flap. With that he recalled some of the carefully-chosen words he'd written for his farewell lecture at Oxford, many years ago:

> Fifty per cent of all barristers are vain and mendacious.
> Truth for them is sometimes disposable: lies are their stock in trade.

Thus corrupted they lie, while calling everyone else liars – usually of the born, confirmed, self-convincing … or of the inveterate variety. The deciding factor between truths and falsehoods for them is, alas, often determined by the size of their spurious glory or undeserved fee. Do not, I beg of you, join them. Avoid them, for they are vexatious to the spirit – as they, alas – use their familiarity with the law to fabricate injustice. The other valiant 50 per cent are besmirched with their vile brush. Your time at Oxford, Ladies and Gentlemen, will have been well spent if you can resolve at all times to keep yourselves free of them. You all know how precarious the dividing boundaries are.

The memory of the composition made him agitated. He tossed aside Dr Humburger's closely typewritten pages and settled down instead to some of the friendly handwritten letters. After a while he took up the Swiss lawyer's letter once more and began to read with a concentration that belied his age.

Then he rang for Webb, took out some private writing paper from his bedside table and scribbled an urgent warning note to his son Charles in France. He was sealing the envelope when Webb came back inside, this time wearing his smart chauffeur's cap with his shoes still smelling of fresh black polish.

"You rang, sir?"

"Webb, you do know Paris, don't you?" Webb looked twice at his master like a canny sheepdog, unsure of whether he'd been given a correct signal. "I was there with you during the war, sir," he replied, still puzzled.

"Isn't it time you refreshed the old memory box, Webb? Charles took off from Oxford Airport in the new jet before 6 a.m. this morning to get to his uncle's lawn meet. Where do you imagine he might be now?"

Webb removed his silver fob watch, given to him by Sir Basil many years before, from his waistcoat. It was 8.30 a.m. "Given the one-hour time difference, he's probably gone to the stables by now to choose his mount. But I know Master Charles will be returning to the family suite at the Hôtel de Crillon late this afternoon. I could await his return there, sir."

Sir Basil nodded approval, amazed once more at Webb's ability to read his mind so accurately. The old man now slid off his bed and allowed Webb to help him dress. Once attired, Sir Basil peered in the mirror and then at the telephone. "Webb, could you get my brother Jacques on the line?"

"I shall try, sir," Webb said eventually, and raised an eyebrow. "I'm having trouble, sir," and handed over the instrument to his master, who said, "The Parisians always do seem so abominably rude on the telephone, Webb. It's just their language, you know. It's terribly curt." Then he mumbled some French into the phone, "Oh, never mind. Thank you."

He turned to Webb again. "The line is down. I'll speak to him this evening." With that, Sir Basil checked his own watch and spoke briskly. "We're off, and we'll just be in time for

College chapel. It's still on for 10 a.m., isn't it?" Hearing Webb grunt assent, Sir Basil and his manservant left the bedroom.

* * *

Outside Sir Basil turned to Webb, who was about to place the heated blankets into the car. "I'll sit at the back of the car this morning. Webb … don't, however, allow Rupert to fiddle with any of the knobs in the front this time." As the Phantom V trundled down the avenue and clattered over the cattle grid one of the ex-Mafia triplets, who was ensconced in the bay window of a weather-beaten stone cottage some distance opposite the main gates, made a quick note of the car's number plates. He then phoned to alert his sibling on his mobile at Heathrow Airport, and ran out to start up his light green hired van so that he could follow in close pursuit.

Chapter Thirteen

In the Lafitte forest Il Perfetto continued to slither underneath the green tarpaulin. The artificial grass cover felt heavy – waterlogged as it was – and covered with snow. As he squeezed himself between it and the rotting grass his nylon fishing jacket hissed serpentlike as he continued to slide down towards the hidden tunnel. But the agony in his chest finally forced him to stop. He groaned through his pale, frozen lips, worried that his one remaining lung might collapse.

The thought of another heart attack also howled in his mind. "Can't afford another one now. Not now," he thought. Il Perfetto knew he needed to sit up, but couldn't. His only chance was to massage his undersized heart (which was the size of a tennis ball) beneath his ribcage. He was already beginning to feel the loss of power in his right hand. Crunching up his fingers and using his fist like a hammer, he massaged his chest with all his remaining strength.

He started to pray now, the instinctive prayer of self-preservation: "God help me now." Soon his thinking was distracted by the thought of the giant fee awaiting them. But could he stave off another heart attack now? As the excruciating pain slowly subsided he felt blood return to his left hand, which was still half clenched on his rifle pouch.

With slow determination he managed to unclench his numb right hand and force his arm sideways. His face brightened as at last he could feel the wet grass give way beneath his body and be replaced by the hard frozen earth dropping down towards the rough, deep tunnel he'd dug out over many long autumn nights. His brain was racing now. He must continue to inch himself forward … and then allow himself to slide down and collapse into the stinking trench.

He winced as a splinter from the wooden lining of the tunnel pierced the soft skin of his trigger finger and his eyes watered. But his face lit up with relief as he welcomed the sensation of real pain.

"Good," he muttered, thinking, "The hideout's so damp now, but stinks with the putrid smell of ------- rat dung." As he stretched his hand forward in the dark, damp tunnel, a soft warm body brushed under the palm of his right hand. "Bloody hell," he screamed, trying to tear his hand away from the warm underbelly of a rat. He felt its tiny feet clinging on to his hand and its sharp, strong ravenous teeth plunging deep into the top of his already-bloodied trigger finger, and was frightened about the eerie vacuum-like sensation as he felt the creature sucking his blood in short energetic bursts. He lashed his hand against the rough wooden sides of the tunnel with muffled cries of panic, and finally dislodged the rat.

"Damn it," he hissed. The seething hatred and desperation in his own voice consoled him as he sucked at his trigger finger, spitting out the contaminated blood as he listened to the pitter-patter of the starving rat scurrying on ahead of him in the damp soil. He felt and smelled the filthy slush in the pitch-black darkness and he shuddered. He gritted his rotten teeth in desperation, sinking deeper into the frozen slush and bruising his elbows as he doggedly heaved himself towards the hollow below the centre of the igloo of cut wooden stakes covered with ice and snow.

Stoically he continued heaving himself through the freezing slime of the narrow tunnel, doubly relieved that his ex-Mafia contact had provided the waterproof fishing gear that morning (he had found it neatly stacked out at the back of his

Ferrari, on top of all his other gear). From the change of air he finally sensed that he was now underneath the centre of the wooden stakes. He twisted his body around in a sitting position and reached up into the hollow mound above him.

"Blast," he shouted, as he felt the incisors of the famished rat savage the tip of his trigger finger again. Gasping in pain – and horrified by the surprise of a second attack – he grabbed the rat with his left hand, tried to throttle its body and flung it down. The rat squealed as it hit the frozen turf and scurried away again. Il Perfetto gritted his teeth as he again sucked on his trigger finger and spat out the blood until no more would come.

Then, gingerly, he reached up again into the hollow of the mound – where his hand knocked against the cold metal base of the tiny canvas chair that he remembered buying in the Bon Marché store some months before. His frozen hand touched the ice-cold aluminium gun support and he shivered, but he knew that everything was as he'd left it. He scrambled up through the narrow hole, pulling his massive rifle pouch up behind him, and carefully stretched himself.

The tiny deckchair squeaked sharply as he dropped down on to it. This was instantly followed by a rasping, grunting sound from his own belly. As the eldest of all the remaining ex-Mafia brothers he was relatively fit and was still in his seventies, but he was also pleased that this was to be his last contract. With the sharp end of his aluminium rifle support he began to chip away at the dull-coloured ice that sealed the wooden stakes. A haze of morning light shafted through as fresh air whistled in. He peered in through the narrow slit in the ice between the stakes.

"Ah. It's snowing again." He sighed gratefully as he took a deep breath, and with relief at the knowledge that his footprints would soon be covered up. He shivered and swore violently at himself. He deserved to be punished for his carelessness in not realising that it can and sometimes does snow in November. Then, squinting in the poor light, he pulled out the thin sliver of wood from his trigger finger. He gnawed again at the punctured flesh, trying to suck and spit out any remaining contamination.

Il Perfetto could feel his trigger finger becoming numb. Quickly he inserted it back into his mouth until it became pliable and sensitive again. With a return of calm professionalism he unsheathed the powerful rifle from its lead-lined fishing pouch and fondly rubbed his hand along its length, feeling the smoothness of the fine wood. He kissed the weapon with pride and recalled arguing with Palermo's finest gunsmith as he'd handed him the log of wood. "Here. Shape the wood from grandfather's olive groves for the butt. Build it as an exact replica of the American Barrett M82A1 12.7, the world's most powerful sniper rifle, with its well-known pinpoint accuracy of over a mile. Then disassemble it."

He now held the glossy butt of the firearm to his lips, closing his eyes as he kissed it in appreciation ... and imagined once again the warmth of his boyhood in Palermo, when he nestled in his grandfather's arms on the pebbly beach of the bay. He reached for the fishing pouch again and removed from it a narrow lead-lined leather tube.

He clicked open the oiled brass combination lock, upending it. His eyes sparkled as he watched the bright Zeiss scope slip down from its pink velvet tubular bed. The adrenalin was flowing freely now, at full tilt, as he thought of the $5 million fee. It warmed his blood. He slotted the Zeiss scope carefully into place, thinking that a silencer over that distance was not on.

Once the technological operations were completed he looked eagerly inside the black rubber cup of the sights and adjusted the gun stand once more. He leaned forward now, feeling the cold rubber cup against the drooping tissue below his right eye and becoming conscious of the sharp damp smell of the rubber cup.

He peered long and hard at the near edge of the snow-covered ice-logged pond one mile away. Continually touching the serrated edge of the tumbler wheel he adjusted the scope more accurately now, almost lazily, until he saw a single crystal of ice dancing on a blade of grass at the edge of the pond ... green, it seemed to him, just like the glinting eye of Jacques, le Comte de Lafitte.

But his exhilaration was brief as he heard his father's cynical voice roaring in his mind again. "You'll only get one damn shot ..." The ex-Mafia don, Il Perfetto's father, had stopped in mid sentence – raising his crooked forefinger and warning him with his cold black eyes as he looked deep into those of his son in spectral admonition – with the final staccato imperative, "Do not mess it up."

Il Perfetto began to perspire again as he recalled the horrid whipping all his triplet brothers had received 12 years ago, after the monumental mess they and al-Qaeda had caused in Oxford. He could still hear the ex-Mafia don roaring at them as he hit them with his thick black leather belt. "Instead of killing Russell-Lafitte you've only crippled him. This contract will probably be abandoned because of your utter stupidity and complete irresponsibility."

The ex-Mafia don had predicted a massive security upgrade to protect the de Lafitte family after that. They would now be more closely guarded than ever. Il Perfetto shivered as he huddled on his flimsy camp seat. He tried to keep warm by stamping his feet. He stared at the moving darkness outside, at the endless rows of trimmed wooden stakes covered with snow that reached out far into the distance of the huge plantation set among thousands of acres of mature beech trees. The swirling mists of frost and the gushing blasts of ice-cold winds continued to season the clusters of converging poles. His eye smarting from the swirling ice-cold vapour, he withdrew his face from the narrow open slit in the ice between the stakes of his igloo.

He'd calculated that today was the only day in the year when le Comte de Lafitte would permit himself to become vulnerable. The banker who controlled the far-flung conglomerate through the de Lafitte Foundation would, as master and huntsman for the day, put on a simple worker's smock, hold a butcher's knife and become a killer. "Just like my ------- self," Il Perfetto thought. He'd allowed, as his father had warned him, for only a single head shot from his Barrett-style rifle. Il Perfetto shivered, feeling the frost penetrate his bones.

"Bloody hell," he spat out in vulgar Italian, got up from his seat, and started a series of quick press-ups. It was all up to him now. Then he started doing more variations of press-ups inside the wooden mound, aware that warming up would make him more fully conscious. He knew it was all up to him now. Soon the whole forest would be alive with the steady drum of horses' hoofs, the resounding of horns and the lively music of hounds. This would be his final assassination, known to him alone, as "The ------- impossible one."

Chapter Fourteen

B eneath the crystal chandeliers in the yellow dining room at Chateau Lafitte Uncle Jacques touched his lips with the starched linen one more time, adding, "That's more or less it, Charles." He carefully refolded his Irish linen napkin before slipping it into an old French silver band. He held it up for Charles to admire. "Papa gave it to me for my first communion. Your grandfather, Charles. A stern but good man. One of the old school." He fondly kissed the family crest etched on the silver ring. "From Papa," he read out loud. "*Soli Deo gloria.*" The crystal chandeliers in the yellow dining room sparkled brightly as breakfast came to an end. Charles and Uncle Jacques looked knowingly at each other for a moment and then at the eight others at table – various French chiefs of police, a de Lafitte director of security, Jacques's private bodyguards – and several other members of the *Sécurité*, whose eyes in turn settled on the two de Lafitte family members.

Jacques made signs of getting up to leave the breakfast table but corrected himself, saying loudly in French, "Grace first."

There followed fast mumblings that echoed round the table of thanksgiving prayers in various languages, which was the cue for the security group to stand up. But Jacques remained seated and leaned over to touch the top of his nephew's hand – which was still resting on the arm of his dining room chair, and looked straight into Charles eyes. "It's entirely your decision, Charles," he whispered softly, "But, given you're a de Lafitte, I've no doubt that you'll instinctively make the right one. Follow me."

Then he reached down, picked up Charles's crutches from the Aubusson carpet and handed them to his favourite nephew. Then he stood upright and said to the others, "Now hurry, you lot. You'll find the rest of your hunting kit in the changing rooms beside the back kitchen, and your hunters are awaiting you in the stables." He looked at his watch and spoke with renewed energy.

"Goodness me. Look at the time. All your mounts must be saddled up by now. You'd best get on quickly. We'll follow." Turning to Charles again – who, meanwhile, had slipped his crutches underneath his armpits – Jacques spoke with merriment in his tone. "I'm afraid your Arab is not available this year, Charles. He's wild. I've allocated him on your behalf to someone very special, whom I should like you to meet." There was a broad grin on his square face as he accompanied Charles through the double door of the dining room – and he added, with a mischievous grin, "I shall formally introduce you to her later." He extended his arm sharply to his right, guiding Charles to a polished mahogany door that led down to the back hall.

"Be careful. Three steps," he reminded Charles as they stepped down on to the bare boards of a semicircular small hall with a huge rounded back door. There was also an adjoining smaller door on one side of the back hall, which he opened. Once inside the boot room Jacques's face hardened as he removed his hacking jacket, switching it for his splendid hunting coat. From its side pocket he pulled out a tiny hand-held tape recorder, holding it up to his nephew.

"Before you finally decide, Charles." He was talking very slowly now, as he held out the tiny tape recorder. "You can hear for yourself what Interpol have been warning us about.

This time we have clear evidence. Listen to this." The old man handed over the miniature recorder to his nephew. Charles, supported by his crutches, adjusted the spindle of the volume control with his forefinger and strained to decipher the words through the static and the interrupted airwaves. The message, in spite of the accented Italian, was unmistakable.

"I presume the whole family will be fully united now and ready, unlike 12 years ago?"

"Yes. We're all in it together now," was the reply in peasant Italian. "Remember, this time you're going for the Count first. Once you get him the rest of the family will rush round like headless chickens. Keep cutting the phone links and you'll be able to pick them off one by one."

"OK."

"There are $1 million for each one of you … $5 million in all – as per the list I emailed to you, with a huge bonus. Start on Saturday: finish by Sunday night."

"OK."

Jacques, too, stared at the tape recorder fixedly, as if he was trying to place one of the voices. He was sure he'd heard the intonation of that voice before, but he couldn't quite place it.

"Interpol intercepted this yesterday," Jacques said. "I know the director. He's a chum of mine. He slipped me this copy yesterday evening over drinks at his place. That's why I immediately phoned your father last night. I was whispering to you from the director's private study, because he's sure it's bugged. What do you think?"

"Yes, I …" began Charles, but Jacques interrupted excitedly.

"They haven't yet positively identified the Swiss voice, but I already have my suspicions. The Italian is reportedly called Il

Perfetto. He's the eldest son of an Italian ex-Mafia family who've been specialising in serial assassinations for many years now. Apparently he has never missed."

"And you're hunting this morning?" Charles asked incredulously.

"I get reports like this every month, Charles. Don't you see? This time we have a decided advantage. It's as if we've received an actual warning."

"But what about the risks you're taking?" Charles looked at his uncle, thinking that either he was too brave or had too high a regard for the French *Sécurité*. Jacques bent down again, dropping the mini recorder into one of his old hunting boots. Then, with a laugh, he looked at his watch again and turned towards the rounded back door. "Our *Sécurité* chaps are riding with us this morning, Charles." As soon as Jacques had said it he himself knew it was a smokescreen. Nonetheless, he turned the great key of the back door and pulled hard. Slowly the massive door began to swing open, moving smoothly, noiselessly.

"After 300 hundred years it still works perfectly," he said, looking keenly at his nephew's face. "That takes skill and time-consuming craftsmanship, which all socialist governments have abandoned. Now they take the waiting out of wanting and they just buy the votes, with wild promises of a university education. They just appeal to glamour, condemning a huge mass of potentially good workers to permanent unemployment." Charles's silence spoke volumes as he raised his eyebrows.

Jacques continued, "All the *Sécurité* boys have already listened to the tape. Interpol told me to take it seriously, because of the involvement of this Italian family." There was a glint in his eye as he looked deep into Charles's eyes. "Tightly-knit families working in harmony have always had to be taken seriously, Charles. That's why I am making a song and dance about it now, and for no other reason." Charles remained silent, as he saw his uncle had not yet finished.

"I gave my secretary instructions yesterday for all my keys to be duplicated, and last night I finished preparing handwritten notes for each of my main files. I even filled in some of Dr Humburger's spare power of attorney forms. He's our company lawyer, based in Geneva. Remember? The chap with those strange, dull-looking eyes."

Jacques stopped. He considered the idea that he'd made the connection with the voice on the tape but he dismissed it instantly, thinking, "How could it be Humburger? He is of the old school." After a brief silence he continued. "I made them out to you and our mutual friend, Charlemagne." Jacques still had his hand on the round knob of the back door. He was looking straight at his nephew.

"All this, Charles, is just in case. It's all there for you to collect at my office in Paris, whenever you want to come on board." He stopped for a moment as he looked fondly at Charles once more, but then continued hurriedly, before Charles could reply.

"Last night I gave only the briefest of outlines to your father. I didn't want to cause him needless anxiety. He's always inclined to worry unduly. But ultimately it's your decision, Charles. Your father would want you to know all the facts before you took any decision. That's his way. What do you think?"

"Don't hunt today," Charles pleaded. "Don't go out today, Uncle Jacques."

"But, Charles, as a family we can't let ourselves be intimidated by rumours about killers or their intentions." Jacques was indignant, but he also sensed the danger. "We have a right to feel secure as we go about our normal business. The police and the *Sécurité* – and, indeed, our own team – are there to protect us. They haven't failed us yet, so far …" He hesitated, remembering the assassination attempt on Charles's life 12 years ago, and he willed himself not to look down at Charles partially-hidden calipers.

He was proud of his nephew as he stood beside him with his crutches, but he regretted his own hesitation as he was about to continue. But now he remembered his brother Guy the inventor – and his wife Anne, who had been murdered in that Chinese cable car accident (so-called). Yes … the actual murder of his close family. Jacques's mouth remained closed. His favourite nephew now raised his voice.

"Your life is in danger now," said Charles with emphasis, reading his uncle's train of thought. "Abandon this hunt, Uncle Jacques. Don't go out today." Charles had raised his voice for the second time, stressing the words as never before, then lowered his tone as he continued. "On Monday announce your immediate retirement and make public the opening for an experienced professional. You must now protect yourself." But, no matter what words he'd chosen, Charles felt how flat it all sounded in this cold morning air. Mere words. It was all too late.

"It should have been done earlier," he thought. All Charles could sense was his own inadequacy. "Ultimately, this is not going to be determined by an exercise in logic. It is now a family thing where normal logic doesn't apply," he decided.

As if reading his mind Jacques suddenly embraced his nephew warmly, planting a full kiss on Charles's left cheek. Then, gripping the ice-covered railings leading down the slippery granite steps at the back of the chateau with his left hand, he placed his right arm around his nephew's waist, lifting him clear of the snow, and took him down the dozen steps down to the snow-covered gravel below. Charles sensed again the warmth and comfort of being part of an extended family. As he pivoted his weight on his two crutches he began forcibly to swing his lower body forward, like a walking pendulum towards the stables, and listened again to the decisive, concluding deadpan tone in his uncle's voice.

"Charles, they'll have one of the Orlov hunters waiting for you with your special saddle from Oxford. It's already late, and we have the master's and huntsman's duties to perform today, but it's good to have our reliable ex-field master back again. In your earlier absence we temporarily appointed a distant family niece, Annabelle – a very much younger field master whose beauty we've no doubt you'll approve of once we've introduced her to you. She kindly agreed to act as our field master 12 years ago and every year in your absence. It's she who wanted to ride your wild Arab again today." He said this quickly with a big grin on his face, looking keenly at his nephew as they entered the long 18th-century stable block.

Charles instantly saw that the Arab's cubicle was empty.

The head groom – who'd been chatting to one of the stable lads – bustled to attend to le Comte de Lafitte, but Jacques sent him instantly over to attend to Charles. He addressed Charles as an old acquaintance but he took note of his crutches. "Monsieur le Comte told me this morning to prepare your Arab for Mademoiselle Annabelle, Monsieur Charles." There was an apologetic tone to his voice as he continued to appraise Charles's enlarged riding boots.

"There's your saddle," he said, indicating to where it lay on a low wooden saddle rack. He then lowered down a set of leather loops – of which Charles slipped one under each armpit – and then Charles allowed himself to be winched up and then down again into the saddle. Once there Charles strapped himself in.

"Good. That feels fine," Charles said. "Up we go." This was the signal for the groom to leave the loops underneath his armpits and to hook up two metal clasps, one on the pommel of the saddle and the other one into a solid metal ring at the back of the saddle, before hoisting the saddle (together with Charles) up in the air again. A stable lad meanwhile brought one of Jacques's steady Orlov hunters underneath, and Charles and his saddle were lowered down to the hunter.

"She wouldn't take 'No' for an answer. No, sir." It was your Arab she was after." The groom continued to chatter as he secured the girth straps. "As soon as she'd laid eyes on him she'd made up her mind." He babbled away in French, looking up at Charles, waiting for a comment. But, receiving no encouragement, he stopped.

"Well done," said Charles. "You've been practising."

"Young fillies are the same the world over," said the groom, ignoring the compliment, adding, "Although this one's exceptional, taking on that wild stallion of yours." Charles detected a note of admiration in his voice and wondered at the groom's parting words as he hacked across the snow-covered park to join the others.

From a long way off through the bare November trees he immediately spotted his Arab stallion, its tail and neck held high in a distinctive arch: the embodiment of a free spirit effortlessly supporting its slim rider, who was mounted on a side saddle. She was as one with the dancing, swinging movement of the Arab.

So this was Annabelle. Charles rode up to take a closer look. So this was the girl who'd spent most of the morning caressing each of the horses in the stables before finally settling on his Arab. Her slender frame was elongated further, since all but a few wisps of her blonde hair were tucked up high above her long neck and rose up into her navy top hat.

Her eyes, the palest of pale powder blue, were partly hidden by her veil ... and fully focused on the staghounds.

Mesmerised by her beauty, Charles followed her eyes – which were brimming with excitement at the movement of the hounds as they rustled eagerly about the snow in a tight circle in front of the chateau (while the stirrup cups were circulating). Soon the French horns sounded, followed by the horn of the master – and the hounds became one surging mass of energy, whose music mingled with the first phase of the sound of the horns. Charles continued to be enthralled and, at the first covert – when the hounds checked, whimpering and wheeling about, in and out of the undergrowth – he continued to watch Annabelle, who stretched her slim body to catch a better view of them. The smooth lines of her well-cut hunting habit accentuated her slender waist and slim bosom.

After miles of galloping he rode up closer still, captivated by the skilled horsemanship with which she controlled the wilful Arab, and was intrigued when he saw the Arab lower his arched neck. The next moment the stallion reared right up on his powerful hindquarters and pawed the air with his front hoofs. Snorting loudly, the Arab's fragile pulsating pink nostrils flared. His round dark glinting eyes rolled. A lesser rider would have been thrown, but Annabelle swiftly brought the stallion back under her control as he lightly touched the snow-covered turf again.

Charles sensed that his broad-hoofed Arab, now nonchalantly mixing the snow with the colourful dead leaves from the damp forest bed, was all hers now. He also realised that he himself was now in danger of being caught, as instinctively she turned to look and flashed him a smile of recognition. In a reflex action Charles raised his top hat, all too aware that he'd never seen such chic elegance before. Who exactly was this beauty?

* * *

Watching through his Zeiss scope, one mile from the ice- and snow- laden pond, the assassin Il Perfetto started to control his breathing so that it was in tune with the murderous rhythm of his mind. But still he refrained from touching the trigger while his inner voice spoke to him. "Something's ------- wrong," it said. Every neuron in his body told him so. "Damn it," he hissed, wondering why the girl in his sights – who was riding side-saddle and wearing a hunting veil – had turned to smile at the rider who was still out of focus some distance behind her.

The assassin now reached up to adjust his sights. He'd seen the vague blur of the rider reaching for his hat in response to her smile. Suddenly he saw, clearly visible, his estranged son's high forehead. "Impossible. It's Il Ragazzo. What's he doing here?" he thought. "He's meant to be in America, handling the Kentucky killings." Il Perfetto averted his eyes, stunned. White with shock, he gritted his teeth. Instinctively he removed the massive weapon from his shoulder.

"What the hell is going on?" he thought. "The many months of meticulous preparation and the $5 million fee for the worldwide elimination of the leaders of the de Lafitte family … was it all now in jeopardy again? Why was Il Ragazzo here today? Did his son perhaps want to send a signal? Does he need help?" Il Perfetto quickly looked at him again through his Zeiss scope and then looked down, again puzzled. "But no. No. This did not fit into my plan. It is wrong. Must think. Must work it out. There is still some time left – and anyhow, the Count must be dealt with first." What could he do? He was here to deal with le Comte de Lafitte.

* * *

The hounds gave tongue as they recovered their line, and Annabelle was right up with them. She was about to follow but hesitated and stole another glance at Charles, suddenly remembering hearing the news 12 years ago that he'd been shot. She'd heard it herself from a distraught Uncle Jacques, who had very reluctantly decided to go ahead with the hunt ball, mainly to spare Charles further publicity. "And here Charles is, hunting with the best of them, the brave fellow," she thought. Did he not doff his hat to her?

Chapter Fifteen

Il Perfetto was certain he had indeed found the weak link in the armour of le Comte de Lafitte. There was a smirk on his face as he continued thinking, "In spite of all the ------- security, the bodyguards, the police, the bulletproof cars and the 24-hour constant surveillance, they're no match for the maestro." The bitterness of Il Perfetto's derision showed on his face, but swiftly he chided himself for this bravado. There was too much at stake. The de Lafitte family were now on their guard. They were very closely-ranked and immensely powerful.

Il Perfetto knew that he shouldn't let emotion get to him. His own family from Palermo had once been powerful in Mafia circles. "But look at us now," Il Perfetto thought. "After the disastrous repercussions of what happened at La Scala in Milan 60 years ago, we had to ------- well slim down: there was no more racketeering – no drugs, no more extortion - just regular, family-executed, overseas assassinations."

Il Perfetto reminded himself that this was to be the last united family contract, with a multiplier bonus mechanism if each member of the family made their hit. In his many lonely moments Il Perfetto had often thought how wonderful it would be if the whole family could retire together to his grandfather's beloved village near Palermo.

But no sooner had that dream entered his mind than he knew it would be impossible. Only he in Europe (together with his estranged son in the USA) had been untouched by the Oxford fiasco.

"My son Il Ragazzo is free from it too," Il Perfetto thought. But he'd lost contact with his boy … and now he turns up here. For years he'd been unable to trace him, until that photograph had arrived two and half years ago. Now here he is today. Every waking moment he'd wondered who'd turned his boy against him. Why, after all those years of family life, could it have so upset the boy? His wife never knew properly about the switch, so he'd assumed that she would not have told him … blurted it out to the boy on her deathbed.

Who else might have told the boy? He could no longer remember exactly when, or feel the actual moment of the rift. It was such a long time ago: his own searing guilt had blurred the details. He only knew the boy now through the ex-don, his own estranged father – and then only on his knees in the ex-don's darkened study in that tax haven. Then only through abjectly whispering into the old man's ear could he get details of his son, Il Ragazzo.

In spite of the early bonding his boy had now become the surrogate grandson of the ex-Mafia don, his own father. But were these not the very reasons why he'd been crawling today in a filthy drain through the slime, the slugs, the stench of the rotting dead and the rat shit, so that his kidnapped son could act as part of the family in this hugely profitable enterprise? So that he might again see Il Ragazzo, his son, however briefly – in the hope that it might finally lead to a reconciliation? Was it true that he'd become a Muslim? How far had he really become involved with that bastard Osama bin Laden and al-Qaeda? Il Perfetto waited for his moist eyes to dry in the rubber cup. He refocused again. His raw forefinger locked on the trigger and tightened.

Where, a nanosecond before, a dancing crystal of dew glistened like a green emerald on a blade of grass at the pond's edge he now imagined he saw – within his mind's eye – a dull charred edge … imagined he had seen it for just a moment, just as in the same manner the liquid emerald had now disappeared. He released the pressure on his trigger finger and then became conscious of his body again, chilled and frozen to the bone. With the resignation of a professional he allowed himself to freeze in these conditions, cold as death, willing himself yet to be ready and able to fix the cross hairs on the forehead of le Comte de Lafitte when the time was ripe.

* * *

Il Perfetto's triplet brothers, the other two of the Tre Terzina, had been given the English side of the morning's killings after endless discussions within the family. "God help them if they failed again," he thought. "Poor bastards."

Chapter Sixteen

The sun's rays were beginning to dapple the snow-laden forest bed, and Charles allowed his steady Orlov hunter to canter on the softer damp ground in the main clearing. In tight formation the large field of hunters churned up the snow and the turf with wild abandon – and now, when he was keeping pace with the main body of horses, he again spotted Annabelle in front. She was right up with the hounds and her finely-tailored hunting habit flexed freely as she leaned forward on her side saddle, gently stroking the Arab's long, arched neck. She'd turned her elegant face – just visible through the netting below her top hat – and cast a glance at Charles, then flung her head away from him.

Outpacing the hounds, the boxed stag disappeared into the undergrowth. The sun flashed streaks of speckled light through the trees on to the snowbound bed of the forest. Charles marvelled at the self-assurance and grace with which she controlled her lively mount. It was if horse and rider were in a lively dance. Briefly Annabelle turned her sculpted face – just visible through the netting below her top hat – towards him, before jerking away again.

She continued to move effortlessly in her tailored side saddle costume and he became doubly fascinated as she and the Arab floated like a gazelle above the ground, seemingly dancing together – the stallion's pink-edged nostrils flaring below the concave profile of his tapered head, all the while carrying his neck in a perfect arc. Annabelle's eyes were on the hounds again as they bustled about, whimpering. He could see from her face that she felt for them, aware that they'd lost their stag.

As they cast about Annabelle again became conscious of Charles looking at her. She glanced at him again, then back towards the pack of hounds, amused, pleased and fascinated by Charles's attentions. She looked around again, opening her eyes wide, urging Charles to recognise her. Then she frowned, puzzled. Why had he not yet realised that she was the girl who'd organised all the others to sit on top of him 30 years ago at a children's party at their Uncle Charlemagne's chateau in Switzerland? It was she who had continued tickling him after all the others had stopped.

Short of telling him, she sensed she could not make him realise that they knew each other and had been childhood friends – but she was determined not to indulge him further. He was so much older now and so handsome, and she wondered why they had not met again in the interval. But it never dawned on her that it was because of her complete transformation into an exquisite beauty that Charles didn't recognise her now. She thought that she'd not changed: she was still the same wild tomboy. She was never getting married, and certainly not to him.

The 12 and a half couple of hounds suddenly gave tongue as they caught the line of an outlier stag. Then they checked again, whimpering, some distance from the marshy pond. Having sent the hounds into cover, Jacques dropped back momentarily to ride beside his nephew. "Her name's Annabelle Beauchamp," Jacques said, chuckling gently. He'd seen his nephew's eyes keenly following the beautiful girl. Then, in a raised voice, so that Annabelle would hear him too, he said, "She's a member of the Scottish branch of Charlemagne's family. Let me introduce you." Jacques's own sudden studied formality caused the old bachelor amusement, and Charles's protests fell on deaf ears. In the French manner,

Jacques turned to Annabelle's mother, who was just behind them.

"Lady Beauchamp, I don't think you've met my English nephew recently: Charles Russell-Lafitte, my original and present trusty field master."

"How do you do? You must be Basil's son. My husband and your father are dear friends. You've surely met my daughter Annabelle," said Lady Beauchamp. She turned proudly to her daughter who tilted her head in acknowledgment, meeting Charles' eyes. With natural grace Charles touched and lifted up his hat, but – uncharacteristically – he didn't smile, as he was overcome by her serene beauty as she lifted up her navy-coloured veil.

As the hounds found their line again Annabelle instantly gave the Arab full rein and flung her head round, but not before her eye had caught Charles's openly-bewildered expression. She still felt his eyes on her but this time she decided not to look around again, suspecting her mother would probably invite Charles to stay for a weekend in the Highlands before the day was out.

* * *

The harsh wind forced wisps of snow into Il Perfetto's smarting eye while he was watching out for his victim, Comte Jacques de Lafitte. He was surprised by the sight of his own son in the company of these strangers. He again worried about his son. "What was he doing here? Had he been lumbered beyond his limits in Kentucky and had come over to ask for help? No, that's not right. He wouldn't do that without contacting the ex-don first, would he? he thought." With that he finally grasped that this handsome young man was not his son but must be the other twin.

"Of course. They're ------- twins. It must be Charles," Il Perfetto thought – the young man he'd instinctively refused to kill 12 years ago. Charles would now be taken care of by the old man, the ex-don, in Paris tonight. "It still feels like killing a member of my own ------- family," he thought bitterly. But what could he do? He needed to fulfil his mission. It was all agreed, and nothing would divert him from the completion of a contract.

Chapter Seventeen

S ir Basil closed his eyes momentarily as they motored past the Leander Club below Henley Bridge, on their way to Rupert's school. He was remembering the spot where he'd proposed to Diana, the eldest of the Russell girl triplets, all those years ago. Then, opening his eyes, he reached for his small well-thumbed address book from his pocket. Removing the car telephone from its small locker beside him in the car he tried to call one of the active bank directors at his home in Geneva, but there was no connection.

He was in no doubt now about the danger facing his brother Jacques. He took out his diary and Dr Humburger's letter from his inside pocket and reread it. Then he wrote a single line on one of the blank blue pages at the back of his Smythson diary and switched on the car intercom.

"Webb, hand me back that letter to Charles I gave you at the house, will you? I want to add something." Sir Basil tore out the small blue page, folding the slip of paper several times along its length into a pointed strip. When Webb handed back the envelope over his shoulder Sir Basil slipped the slim wedge of paper inside the already-sealed back flap of the envelope. "Make sure you hand it to Charles yourself this evening, Webb," he said, handing back the envelope. "Yes, sir," said Webb, lifting his chin, catching the eye of his old master, and he pocketed the envelope once more. Webb pointed playfully at Rupert's finger, which was poised to touch one of the many small knobs on the polished dashboard.

"Don't touch." Webb mouthed the words silently, with a grin, as they took a slip road off the motorway and finally approached the Eton playing fields. Sir Basil looked across the road to the simple triple-beamed wooden gate set into a hedge, which led into the field called Agar's Plough.

He closed his eyes again, recalling the first time he had set eyes on the Russell triplets. It was 4 June, a long time ago ... sunny, unlike today. His sister had pointed them out to him. Like his own sister, they were all wearing St Mary's school uniforms. A little girl wearing pigtails called Diana caught his eye. She was lounging on the grass while her younger triplets occupied the picnic rug. She was such a pretty girl – a world apart from his own dry world of a young Oxford don. Sir Basil always remembered her like that, in a light blue and white gingham dress set off against the darker green of the freshly-cut summer grass. Her pink limbs and blonde hair shimmered in a blaze of sun as she squabbled pink-cheeked with her siblings over the last remaining strawberry.

Sir Basil caught further occasional glimpses of her as she grew up. She continued to intrigue him as she floated through his life, so near and yet so far away from his own so-called reality. When she was up at Oxford as an undergraduate they spoke to each other only with their eyes, without sound. They sensed each other without the need to touch or even breathe the air in which they dreamed, knowing each other without direct knowledge, trusting in other restful spirits to unite their souls. Diana was the happiest and most carefree of the triplets, which was unusual for an eldest child. This had made it all the more difficult for her acquaintances to comprehend her subsequent decision to go out with Basil, an Oxford don, an academic – a virtual recluse. The general vacuum which followed the departure of the famous Russell girls from the Oxford scene was marked by Diana's newly-acquired simplicity, when later she became Basil's wife.

Sir Basil suddenly opened his eyes, and thought about his son Charles who – to the best of his knowledge, like himself at that age – had not the slightest notion of getting married. With sadness folding his eyelids he worried about the young man's awful crippling injury and thought about his distant niece, Dr Caroline Conolly-Lafitte. "Was she still in Bogota, South America? Caroline was about Charles's age. Must try and get in contact with her and arrange a meeting. She's a good girl and a very distant cousin," he thought.

"Stop at the Burning Bush," he reminded Webb, and leaned forward to address Rupert. "Mind you keep your scarf well tucked into your coat. We don't want another setback, do we?"

Rupert quickly opened the door of the Rolls. "Grandpa, I'll be on top of the wall with my friends after Lower chapel. I'll be looking out for you." He closed the heavy front door of the vintage motor and was about to run off but stopped, turned and quietly knocked on the side window of the Rolls, which the old man lowered.

"Thank you for coming. I love you, Grandpa," he whispered very seriously, before running the short distance to his House. Sir Basil watched him proudly, following his every movement. His face clouded as he thought of how isolated the boy must feel, being foreign. Perhaps it wasn't so unlike Diana's case when she'd married him, an Oxford don. He smiled as he remembered how soon they'd ceased to be a topic of conversation once their contagious happiness had encouraged an ever-wider circle of friends, right up to Diana's sudden death giving birth to the twins – of whom, according to the records available, only Charles had survived. It had only been possible for Sir Basil to absorb that double shock because he'd already become one with Diana in the calm acceptance of all seemingly inexplicable tragedies.

At the zebra crossing near the main school quad Webb made a U-turn, but waited for a heavily-tanned man to cross the road. He wore a white bow tie, was dressed in a morning suit like most of the other beaks and was carrying a violin case in his white-gloved right hand. Sir Basil praised his manservant.

"Well done, Webb. We'll make our own way home. It's Rupert's short leave, you know. Stop here." As Basil started to climb out of the car at the entrance to the main college quad he spied one of his former school chums walking past him on the wide footpath.

"Boozy? Boozy, is that you?" His former boyhood friend seemed not to hear. Sir Basil repeated himself, in a louder voice. "I say, Boozy. Fancy you still being around. Why not come and join my grandson and me at the wall game after chapel?"

"C-can I? Jolly decent, B-Bazz. What f-fun." As they made their way towards chapel Sir Basil noticed that Boozy still had his stutter. "I say, B-Bazz, let's sit together ... You know, where we always sat in the old d-days, w-what?"

They turned right inside the quad, then right again. The drops of moisture in their eyes multiplied as they walked up the oak stairs. They ran their fingers over the black oak banisters, aware of the loud creaking of the warped steps. Soon they were up in the marbled entrance. They proceeded past the stalls reserved for the choirboys and continued on into the main body of College Chapel. They sat down near the tall bronze lectern on the left. Sir Basil stared at the wall to his right – his eyes wandering, as in his youth – to the characters depicted in the 16th-century Flemish wall murals.

Chapter Eighteen

M eanwhile, hidden behind an arras in the organ loft, the darkly-tanned man wearing the white bow tie was now bending over his violin case – and opening the silent lock from which, many years before, he had removed the spring from the locking clasps. He lifted out three separate mechanical pieces in turn, sliding them silently into each other without as much as a hint of a clicking sound.

Il Terzina looked stone-faced at his assembled weapon Partially by instinct – but mainly through recent rigorous training – he checked everything again, and then went over everything a third time. He was somewhat surer of himself after the period of low confidence following the fiasco in Oxford. He was about to start adjusting his telescopic sight but stopped to listen to audible footsteps.

"Bloody hell. Footsteps coming up from below, up along the narrow wooden spiral staircase," he thought. The eldest (by three minutes) of the Italian ex-Mafia triplets froze. He swivelled his eyes around and down, checking that the curtain was properly drawn. The footsteps were getting louder. They'd reached the top of the stairs, coming closer ... Suddenly they stopped, right in front of the curtain.

"Bloody hell. Bound to hear my heart booming louder and louder inside the hollow of my chest, like a booming ------- drum. The organist, or whoever it was, is bound to hear it. The curtain's quivering. That's his ------- hand appearing at bottom of the arras. Is he going to whip up the curtain?"

Il Terzina braced himself, not daring to look down. The grip on his still-empty rifle tightened. His face glowing with beads of perspiration, he readied himself to use his weapon as a battering ram. His chest was about to explode as the ex-Mafia assassin asked himself, should he stand on his toes now, ready to use all his strength. No. Mustn't make a sound. He'll hear the slightest creak."

The sound of paper scraping on the bare floorboards came as a relief, but Il Terzina's chin quivered as he lowered his eyes down again towards his feet as he heard the organist scrape up a loose sheet of music from the floor. His intensive training under his brother Il Perfetto prevented him from sighing as he heard the footsteps move away, on and on, relaxing him further, until he heard the music stops of the organ being pulled out. With the first tentative sound of the near-silent air motors being warmed up he felt less on edge.

"Bloody hell. That was close. Best insert the earplugs before the organ gets going," he thought. The photographs of his intended victim lying in his open violin case were superfluous now. It was impossible that the slim man sitting down below the bronze lectern could possibly be anybody else but Sir Basil Russell-Lafitte. The monocle in his left eye alone was a giveaway. Il Terzina continued to fine-tune his telescopic sight, focusing between the target's left ear and eye. But he'd already noticed from his vantage point in the loft that part of Sir Basil's head remained hidden by the top end of the bronze lectern.

Remembering the ex-don giving him and his other twin another heavy warning two nights ago, he thought he'd play it safe and wait. After having given his sworn oath to his father that he would never again take stupid risks and would only go for clean head shots he would never want to go through all that again.

There was a hushed disturbance down below as the Provost in his black robes entered the chapel. He and his few guests sat down in the carved wooden pews on the right-hand side below the organ loft. The solemn music from the thundering organ filled the Henry VI chapel – and the choirboys, wearing white surplices over crimson gowns – emerged singing from the antechapel, and progressed through the choir stalls in double file.

Il Terzina now fitted the giant silencer to his rifle. Then he reached down again to his violin case and lifted one of the invisible flaps, which revealed a small cubicle in the centre. From this he picked up a single transparent surgical glove. He removed the white cotton glove from his right hand and then silently put on the surgical glove. Then his left hand prised open another flap in the orange velvet bed of the violin case. With his surgically-gloved hand he removed one of the two silver bullets from the secret compartment. He held up the handmade Italian silver bullet, his brown eyes glistening with concentration as he peered at the poison-filled ridges at the tip of its head. He pursed his lips into a silent, distant kiss and inserted the ammunition into the breech. "Seek him out, my cunning one," he silently mouthed. Then he waited.

At 10.30 a.m. precisely, prayers over, the trumpet voluntary sounded. The choirboys led the way out of the chapel in double file. The Provost and his guests exited from the place of worship and congregated briefly in the marble antechapel. The schoolboys in their black tailcoats, commemorating the mourning of King George III, had already stood up, as had their proud parents, grandparents and godparents. So too had Sir Basil and his old school chum, Boozy, both with tears of joy in their eyes.

Il Terzina reduced the rhythm of his heartbeat. His face froze as he sensed the pressure of the trigger on his index finger. He'd started to squeeze, holding it there on a razor's edge, waiting for the exact moment when the organ blasts would drown the muted sound of his silencer.

No, not yet. Just a fraction more … Yes … Now. Il Terzina did not allow his right eye, shielded in the black rubber cup of the telescopic sight, to deviate even a fraction as he coldly observed the fruition of his deadly work. He continued to stare at the scarcely-visible bullet hole in Sir Basil's silver locks. Only when he was satisfied did he catch breath again, but he continued to watch the tiny hole left by the silver bullet. Few saw Sir Basil collapse into his dumbfounded friend's arms. Only when the perplexed Boozy lowered the lifeless body of his friend did the first trickle of poisoned blood darken Sir Basil's white hairs.

Il Terzina kept watch, waiting to see the results of the poisonous compound at work. His lips quivered when he saw Sir Basil's neck snap back with a convulsive and horrid finality. When it remained locked in that position he knew that the first stage of his mission was complete. Silently he peeled off the surgical glove, exchanging it with the white one. He dismantled the weapon and reinserted it piece by piece into the velvet-lined compartments of the violin case. He double-checked that everything had been put back into the violin case and then removed his earplugs, becoming suddenly conscious of the loud trumpet blasts of the organ.

Though aware that the organist was still a danger to him, he felt reassured in the knowledge that as long as the music continued he was safe. On tiptoe he stole his way to the spiral staircase before making good his escape down the spiral stairs.

Although he was in a hurry he mingled nonchalantly with the parents on their way out of the chapel. He was careful not to make eye contact with the headmaster, who was occupied with bidding his farewells to parents as they made their way through the antechapel. Once away from College buildings there was still one more duty to perform, which he did with alacrity. Soon the telephone wires to the outside world were severed which, combined with the major computer crash on the eastern seaboard in America, would ensure further lack-of-communication chaos.

Meanwhile, the stir in the chapel did not prevent the general move towards the wall game, which was getting under way.

Chapter Nineteen

T he youngest of Tre Terzina triplets took exactly six seconds to pick the lock of Matron's Tower which overlooked the wall game. From the top of the snow-covered flat roof of the tower he was able to see the full length of the dull red brick wall.

"------- sitting ducks," he thought, as he saw some more boys climbing to the top of the wall that overlooked the ancient field of grass. The other side of the wall formed part of the public roadway into Eton town. Where they played the wall game it was (on the near side) parallel to the wall and just over a pitch wide. Along the length of the pitch a narrow line of wooden planks had been set out for parents and friends to stand on.

Il Terzina squatted down in the fast-disappearing snow for his press-ups. After 15 minutes of non-stop exercise he rolled over, perspiring gently. He lay on his back on top of the quickly-drying roof, staring up at the sun-splashed November sky. In a playful mood, he stretched his arms over his head and opened his violin case. With cupped hands he lifted out two sections of his rifle and held them aloft over his chest against the sun's autumn rays. Then he lowered them down to his face, smelling the olive wood of the butt and gently wiping the breech against his cheek before assembling the two parts of his rifle. The noise from below started to grow louder. He snapped himself up into a yoga squatting position.

"Bloody hell. What's happening?" he thought. Had he missed anything? Quickly assembling the remainder of the rifle, complete with its long Milanese silencer, he listened calmly to the first cheers (which heralded the arrival of the Scholars) and then watched greedily as the Collegers charged on to the pitch. Meanwhile the boy Rupert and his chums jostled each other as they too rushed to scramble up the small metal rungs inset into the road side of the brick wall. They were less than 300 yards from College Chapel. As soon as Rupert's blond locks appeared over the top of the wall Il Terzina sighted him, double-checking his prey with the aid of many photographs.

There was no mistaking the boy but he checked again – and again, and a third time – through his telescopic sight. It had taken him a long time to acquire the same thorough approach as his father and older brothers. Satisfied that everything was as it should be he allowed himself to become entranced by the fun the boys were having as – with legs astride – they jockeyed along the high wall, peering down from their precarious vantage point, laughing and joking.

Suddenly there was a respectful silence as the opposing team of senior Oppidan players clambered over the same section of the wall, jumped down – and limbered up to confront the Collegers, all scholarship boys. Il Terzina found the preliminary formalities amusing but watched, fascinated, as the Collegers' scrum rammed into that of the Oppidans.

The two sides of the scrum brimmed with energy but with little movement, in a constant unending sequence of crablike activity. They heaved and pushed against each other, trying to avoid scraping their faces against the old rough brick of the wall. Mud-ingrained gloves (finding tender eyes and ears) moved in slow motion from the scrum from time to time, with the steaming ruck scarcely moving more than a few inches forwards or backwards.

As the scrum eventually floundered and broke up Il Terzina could readily identify with the ferocity of the game. He saw that it wasn't so different from the football pile-ups he'd enjoyed as a boy on the streets of Palermo. He continued to watch with fascination as the mud churned up by the studded boots of the warring parties became part of each boy's mud disguise. The snow-covered green turf underneath the two camps rapidly disappeared, congealing inch by inch into one gigantic, moving mound of mud along the rough brick wall. Il Terzina suddenly came out of his reverie when he heard the high-pitched shouts of encouragement that came from the top of the wall.

"Come on, Oppidans." His Zeiss scope instantly zoomed and fell on Rupert's youthful face again. It remained locked on. The scholarship supporters, facing the wall in one long, stretched-out formation, started to call out each letter of College individually – and, with that, Il Terzina knew that soon the killing moment would be at hand. After a huge roar after the last letter: that would be his moment. His face set, but he had not yet started to slow down his heart rate. He would wait until the chorus reached the letter G. Il Terzina was no longer distracted by the other boys' eager faces.

His Zeiss scope was steadily focused on that smooth section of hair and flesh between Rupert's ear and eye. Rock steady, he began to squeeze the trigger as the Collegers began to approach the letter G. The roar after the last letter E – at its most triumphant, and drowning out all other sounds – was the signal for Il Terzina to apply just a little more final pressure on the trigger.

"Phutt." Il Terzina heard the exit from his silencer after he watched the boy's face exploding like a pink watermelon. What remained of the boy instinctively seemed to reach for his missing forehead. His body glanced sideways against one of his bewildered friends before tumbling down the roadside of the wall. As yet oblivious to the assassination of the youngest member of the de Lafitte family the scrummage continued before the faint cries of Rupert's friends, some of whom had instantly jumped down to attend to him, became audible.

By that time two of the Tre Terzina triplets were already in their green van, driving to their next assignment in Oxford.

Chapter Twenty

M eanwhile in Paris that Saturday evening Charles's sister Anne watched the lights on the Avenue Foch being switched on. Secure in her town house, she was nonetheless somewhat surprised that neither Charles nor Uncle Jacques had phoned her after the stag hunt. She felt an involuntary moment of concern, but consoled herself it was all being saved for her drinks party later that evening. Then – as they often did – her thoughts strayed to her son Rupert, whom she truly loved more than she could ever find time to explain fully to the boy.

Daddy, as always, was right. Divorce at any time with Jean-Pierre would be devastating for poor Rupert. She resolved to talk to Charles as soon as she had the chance: 12 years ago, when she'd joined the public relations department of the de Lafitte group after the accidental death of her favourite Uncle Guy and his wife (on the same day as the shooting of her brother Charles in Oxford) she'd felt the need to be more involved in whatever was happening around her, particularly as her Uncle Jacques had instantly offered her the ideal position. She had also, meanwhile, had a little time to spend with her distant cousin Dr Caroline Conolly-Lafitte in South America – in (of all places) Bogota, a run-down city where human life was on a par with vermin in the rat race of survival.

Poor Caroline. Anne had been left feeling it was a waste of a beautiful girl in the world's worst slum. She'd even mentioned her exquisite beauty to Charles but (while it just about seemed to register with him) she dismissed the thought as she compared Charles with her own father – who had been himself still a bachelor at 40. "Caroline should be here with us, hunting with Uncle Jacques at our lawn meet," she thought.

"At least we here in France are still free from the media in London, where everyone since the Labour party came into power has been made to feel guilty – and are perhaps beginning to feel differently – about hunting. It would take some time for the Conservative party – in spite of their promises – to bring the whole complexity of a new bill before parliament, because of the huge debt created by the Labour fiasco.

"No amount of political correctness, however, will alter our inbred French bond with country ways … with the change of seasons, which brought about the hunting of the fox and other vermin as a protection in preparation for spring lambing. It also gives us the occasion to celebrate with the country poor, who could never afford to venture into the costly cities for their enjoyment. What made city folk so bitter about simple, age-old country enjoyments, when hunting had been such a practical and inexpensive way of dealing with vermin for hundreds of years?" Anne thought.

An old copy of *Forbes* magazine lying on the bright yellow carpet of her bedroom caught her attention. She picked it up, absent-mindedly flicking through it, until she saw a photograph of her Uncle Jacques, the insert she herself had secured, which again she checked:

Extension of Lafitte-Para-continental Holdings

Para-continental, the subsidiary of Lafitte Holdings, pursuing the extension of their activities near Chicago, have recently announced the decision to erect a high-capacity steel plant.

Funds will come from within the group and it is not intended to go to the market. Present in New York was the US and intercontinental chairman

Jacques, le Comte de Lafitte, telling the meeting that it was intended that the additional capacity would be available within one year.

Anne, still holding the magazine, took the telephone from her bedside table and sauntered with it towards the adjoining bathroom. She placed the telephone on the corner of the bath, which had been run for her, and felt the temperature of the water. She was still drowsy from her jet lag and her afternoon nap. She tested the water with her hand, letting the silk dressing gown slide from her slim, tanned body.

She settled herself in the water before picking up the telephone receiver. The line was dead, but she seemed not unduly concerned. It explained why she had not been disturbed by a single telephone call while she was asleep. Her loyal chambermaid had directed the cleaning contractors herself that morning, in preparation for that evening's cocktail party following Anne's prolonged stay in New York.

She consoled herself that at least one of her friends or neighbours would report the telephone. It probably has something to do with the rumoured US computer crash she'd heard about on the refurbished *Concorde* as she flew over from New York. Again, Anne examined carefully the photograph of her uncle, with whom she had developed a good working relationship - especially once he'd given her the company gold card to use for all her entertainments, which was a wonderful way of coping with the world credit crunch that seemed to be getting worse day by day.

Then she threw the magazine on the floor and rubbed the sleep from her eyes. It wasn't work at Jacques's company that was bothering her that day: she thought again about her telephone call earlier in the week from New York, informing her father of her intention to divorce Jean-Pierre. Her father

Basil had remained silent for such a long time. There was a seriousness to his voice when he'd finally said, "Anne, we are all heirs to God's kingdom, unless of course we consciously insist on denying our inheritance."

He'd remained silent again for such a long time after that, until she really thought he wasn't going to say anything further – and she'd said, "Pappa?" With that she'd heard him clear his throat and say, "Divorce is a grievous contravention of God's law. A clear denial, Anne, and liberal priests and bishops are not empowered to make it less so. I would ask you to pray and reflect carefully upon it. You should be aware that you will commit a mortal sin if you go ahead with it, unless you get a formal annulment from Rome – and that will take time and is never a foregone conclusion." There was another pause, then he'd added, "But I love you, darling," which prompted him to add, "Speak to Charles about it."

That night in New York she'd cried herself to sleep, convincing herself that her father's religion was of the old school ... though he was probably right, as he was an academic who very much kept up to date with the Church's teachings rather the vested information of the self-styled specialists. He kept his own counsel and prayed about contentious subjects.

Pappa always chose to avoid the in crowd, whom he referred to as "The men of the world". She too, was suspicious of that crowd, yet she knew in her heart that no matter what advice Pappa chose to give her she'd have ended up doing whatever pleased her at the time. But she was always sure to get an honest answer from her father, no matter what the crisis. He'd never taken an active role in the family's holdings, but he had rather encouraged her and her brother Charles "To give it a try someday."

She so loved Pappa ... "But why then do I feel so far removed from him and his views?" Anne thought. "Why has life become so impossible?" Anne had asked herself that question so many times throughout the past few years, particularly when Jean-Pierre was away working on his career in New York and Tokyo. That and losing her favourite godparents, Uncle Guy and Auntie Anne, in a freak cable car accident while on a skiing holiday in China 12 years ago.

That tragedy resulted in Anne crying herself to sleep most nights. Poor Uncle Guy, the nuclear scientist and chief inventor for the family – who, with his wife, had virtually adopted her as their own. When still young, Guy had married Anne St Julien – the daughter of the fifth-generation Swiss chocolate manufacturers. He'd been working in the Lafitte family foundation's laboratories in Geneva on a revolutionary development in nuclear energy, but he'd never allow himself to talk about it except to his own brothers, in particular to Jacques.

After the as-yet-unresolved cable car accident at the time Charles had been shot in Oxford, Guy and Anne's only child (called Marie St Julien-Lafitte) had been adopted by all her cousins, but especially by Charles and Anne. Poor Marie. It had only been 12 years ago when Uncle Jacques had taken on the extra burdens of Uncle Guy's responsibilities: that was when Anne committed herself to undertake some of the public relations work. That's really when her difficulties with Jean-Pierre started, too.

"Funny, that. Contradictory, really," she thought, as she got out of the bath, wrapping herself in a huge bathrobe. She hugged herself and wondered again why life had become so impossible. She stared at herself in the steamed mirrors of the bathroom, thinking again, "Life's really impossible and yet Pappa and Charles are always so happy." She must really talk to Charles tonight.

Chapter Twenty-One

E arlier that same day, deep in the Lafitte forest, Il Perfetto observed through his Zeiss scope that the stag's brilliant gliding movement had, after 12 noon, stiffened to a haggard, strutting helplessness. Each time the animal floundered its jaws locked yet more firmly together. "It won't be long now," the assassin thought.

* * *

Later that afternoon the hunt was indeed approaching its end. Charles noticed Annabelle and her mother leave before the kill. They had talked earlier about catching the evening flight from Charles de Gaulle to Edinburgh. Clearly they weren't going to put themselves out just to indulge in the flesh-pressing and junketing, Charles concluded. Then he remembered that he'd promised to attend his sister Anne's drinks party in the Avenue Foch before flying out to Scotland himself that night. If he was going to get there he had to go now, so he raised his gloved hand to Jacques, who had eyes only for the stag. *"Bonsoir,"* Charles said, before moving off with a small party of friends.

As soon as they arrived back at the stables (while the others were feeding their horses sugar cubes before handing them over) Charles invited the small party into his Bentley before entering the stables himself, in order to allow himself to be dismounted with the help of the head groom. Letting the groom take charge, he considered the worrying conversation with his father earlier that day and Uncle Jacques's brave, unwavering attitude towards all forms of threats. What if the assassins carried out their plan against Uncle Jacques in the next few weeks? Who then would be the driving force at the de Lafitte bank and at the Foundation? Who would take care of the de Lafitte stake in the Wall Street investment houses, in China's largest mines and steel plants, in USA property companies – and in that most advanced nuclear research and development company based in Geneva?

Charles knew it would take him many years to acquire Uncle Jacques's know-how, even as a full-time understudy. Why hadn't he appreciated that his own Uncle Jacques was merely being kind and honourable by being so scrupulously fair in allowing him to make up his own mind at his own pace? "Why," he asked himself, "Have I not made it absolutely plain about the necessity of a de Lafitte family member to hold the delicate balance of power between Steere's bank and the gifted shares of the Vatican bank's holding in *Aligoté Nucleaire SA*? Why had not Uncle Jacques stressed it more – made it clearer to me – that the Nuclear Arms Treaty Club (NATC) would be rudderless without at least one de Lafitte understudy in position?"

As things stood today it was clear that the Chinese had secretly built their latest 094 nuclear submarine at the Sanya naval base on Hainan Island in the South China Sea only a few hundred miles from Hong Kong. Why did they need a huge network of totally undetectable tunnels capable of holding large numbers of nuclear submarines? The West was now dangerously exposed to the Chinese Nuclear Acquisitions Peace Programme (CNAPP), which sought to fill any possible void in their nuclear know-how. In a worst-case scenario this could lead to a nuclear holocaust in the second or third decade of this new millennium.

Charles couldn't ascertain the full implications of the possible chaos and he was angry with himself for not recognising what his uncle had been trying to tell him all those years ago. Why had he taken all this time to get the measure of Uncle Jacques's generosity and kindness? Yes, the announcement Uncle Jacques had made at the hunt ball 12 years ago must have been an indicator of the timing he'd envisaged – instead of which Jacques had had to wait, ploughing on by himself, regardless.

As he took his crutches from the head groom Charles blushed at the very thought, realising more fully now what had been expected of him. As he left the stables on the way to the car he made a firm moral commitment there and then to change his strategy. As he began to squeeze himself in behind the especially-modified steering column of the Bentley he realised that this would be his last free weekend.

He heard his friends comment, "Charles you're very quiet," but before dismissing everything from his mind he'd resolved that after the next Kentucky weekend he would make an appointment with Uncle Jacques to visit Uncle Charlemagne in Switzerland. Following which, after a further talk with his father, he would give up his present studies in theology at St Benet's Hall in Oxford and give his full attention to the family.

* * *

Back in the Lafitte forest Il Perfetto the seventy-five-year-old assassin reminded himself that he had never failed to complete a contract. He felt cold and was aware he was past his best form, but at least he had the confidence of never having missed. This always comforted him. Yet each night in his dreams he relived again the downfall of his family shortly after the Second World War nearly 70 years ago, outside the opera house of La Scala de Milano.

He'd never been able to erase that gruesome scene of his boyhood: witnessing down below in the square his older brother being gunned down, together with all his uncles. It had left a hungry scar, forever being fed by his rampant imagination. Il Perfetto could still remember the angry vibration in his father's grip as the don had grabbed him from behind while he stood tiptoe on a chair which overlooked the plaza. The don had dropped his gun on the blood-red cover of the chair on which the young Il Perfetto (still in short trousers) was standing.

His father's firm leathery left hand had clamped down over his mouth to stop him screaming – and with his right hand he held back both Il Perfetto's arms, which prevented him from bashing in the window of the balcony on which they both stood. For 10 long, shuddering minutes the pair had witnessed the torment in riveting silence. Ever since Il Perfetto had never failed to plan and prepare his ground over and over, until all chance elements were eliminated.

His first notable implementation of his attention to detail was the successful assisted execution of Roberto Calvi at Blackfriars Bridge after the Archbishop Marcinkus affair. It had taken him many years to prepare for today's operation, but Il Perfetto was certain that his procedure was the only method which would bring success. It was the inherent insecurity of his certainty which, added to the flow of adrenalin, was keeping him warm enough to operate effectively. Still haunted by the cry of the hounds he tried to remain calm, aware that they always had this unsettling effect on him however far away they were.

After years and months of thorough practical research the international dimension of The de Lafitte Protocol stretched wide, and was all-embracing. Meticulous planning always had the effect of relaxing Il Perfetto. He was fully aware that within his planning he could always vary his moves at a moment's notice and, so far, he had personally never failed. Yet through the gushing blasts of the ice-cold wind he shivered as he heard again the semblance of other faint sounds which mingled with those never-ending, eerie notes of the de Lafitte hounds.

He shivered again as he experienced another throb of uncertainty, feeling uneasy as he balanced himself on the tiny canvas chair while he hid underneath one of those clusters of seasonings which formed part of the endless, converging poles in the clearing in front of him. In his mind the snow now transformed those stacks into ghostly igloos. He cursed himself on losing his concentration, as he had to refocus again on the task he'd set himself. With renewed attention, yet freezing in his bunker in the forest, Il Perfetto tried in vain to interpret the music of the hounds.

"Those damned animals are getting closer all the time. Bloody hell," he cursed again out loud, with hatred in his voice. Through his Zeiss scope he'd caught a fleeting glimpse of the stag in the covert, with the hounds not far behind. He adjusted his seating once more, and through his powerful scope he saw the dark outline of the stag set off against the snow-covered ground. He thought, "It won't be long now before he seeks sanctuary in the icy waters of the pond."

Il Perfetto knew he was taking a risk in adjusting his telescopic sight again. "Yes … There they are again, those massive giant antlers." He kept on looking at the size of them: they were held low, just above the ground, relentlessly bruising and jostling with the young leafless willows near the edge of the pond. Il Perfetto continued to adjust his sights until he could see the exhausted stag with rolling eyes wearily forcing himself through the remains of some dead bracken and frozen briars.

He watched the frenzied animal emerge, bellowing and cracking the brittle thin sheet ice as he staggered into the frozen pond.

From a full mile away Il Perfetto sensed it all now, feeling for the beast as if he was right there with the stag. Il Perfetto forced himself to ignore the ice-cold drip from the icicles melting above his head. It had been like this for several hours, but these were the vital moments and he couldn't afford to lose focus for even one second. As he watched what had been a nimble, agile beast glide into the icy waters he twitched, identifying with the sideways-lurching stag, and noticed from its rolling eyes that it had even become frightened of its own shadow. Then suddenly – with a pitiful roar – the animal turned to face its pursuers and raised its head, standing at bay in the icy waters.

Il Perfetto sensed the stag would soon be put out of its misery by the master huntsman, Jacques le Comte de Lafitte – his victim – who was not far behind. Meanwhile he continued to watch the staghounds in close pursuit, thrashing about in the ice-logged water, steaming and trembling with exhaustion. Some of the lighter hounds balanced themselves on as yet unbroken ice. With hind legs apart they stopped themselves from slipping as they strained their necks, throwing tongue in short, victorious bursts.

The icicles above his head kept on steadily dripping water on Il Perfetto's neck – but he reminded himself to make little of it, that it would be like this for only a little longer. Time for him now consisted of these present seconds: these vital, sequential, never-ending moments. He told himself again, "Can't afford to allow the eyes to lose focus for a split instant." No need to worry about anything else, since the storm was blowing itself out. The wind strength, that most variable drag factor determining the bullet's flight over a mile, would no longer be of any consequence. Il Perfetto felt that his wait was about to come to an end. It was all or nothing now. His right eye (within the soft rubber cup of the Zeiss scope) now focused on the man dressed in the dark blue jacket with the red and gold lapels of the master.

The sun was sinking fast, but Il Perfetto kept le Comte de Lafitte firmly in his sights. He observed him loom up on horseback to the very edge of the pond. He watched him dismount, then saw him reach up to his saddle to remove a cream-coloured roll of cloth from one of the saddle pockets. He watched him unfold it, gently shake it and then tie the huntsman's apron strings securely around his angular body.

Il Perfetto followed le Comte de Lafitte with his right eye as he strode down into the icy waters in his highly-polished black leather riding boots with their distinctive mahogany-coloured leather top above the knee. It seemed to Il Perfetto that he could actually hear the thin slivers of ice at the edge of the pond cracking under the aristocrat's weight. Then through his high-powered telescopic sights Il Perfetto watched his victim, a killer like himself, unsheathe a long killing blade with his right hand.

Suddenly le Comte de Lafitte lurched forward, grasping the butt of the stag's right antler with his left hand. Grimacing, he thrust the long blade low down, deep and upwards with his right hand. Again he pushed it deeper yet through the stag's matted crop, slicing through the animal's heart.

* * *

Even from that distance Il Perfetto sensed what must have been a brittle moment of silence as each of the hunt member's faces tensed — each of them waiting for the stag's jaws to snap open, ejecting speckles of blooded saliva flying through the air and staining the huntsman's pristine smock.

Il Perfetto's eye in the sniper scope was rock steady. "Madonna, this is it," he thought as he continued to chew his damaged forefinger, feeling the pain caused by his yellow teeth pummelling the very nerve ends of his trigger finger. He stopped before any tears watered his eyes.

He watched le Comte de Lafitte pull out his gory knife and saw the stag shuddering. A tense moment, as Il Perfetto imagined he could hear the stag's antlers rattling, sinking down ... dying among the fungus-covered roots into the murky water of the pond. Il Perfetto now placed his raw, sensitive forefinger lightly on the ice-cold trigger. His killing moment had arrived. He smiled grimly and reduced the rhythm of his heartbeat. He held his breath as he started to squeeze.

"Come on, you bastard. Raise your head just a fraction more. Come on." Just another fraction into the upper quartile of the Zeiss scope's cross hairs. "Slowly now," he whispered. "Very slowly ..."

Chapter Twenty-Two

"Yes …" A loud thunderclap shattered the air, rolling around from hill to dale for miles about. Il Perfetto – with his cold unwavering eye clamped inside the rubber of his Zeiss scope – allowed himself to feel the vibration of steel and olive wood in his hands and the recoil of the butt of the sniper rifle on his shoulder as he smiled with satisfaction.

* * *

Le Comte de Lafitte flew sideways out of the water as the assassin's high-velocity bullet pulverised his face, lacerating his eyeballs … and deeper yet inside, the vaults of his brain.

He sensed … while scrambling, his neck snapping back … a terrible lightning, with the evacuation of tissues exiting with loose bone fragments mixed with cerebrospinal fluid – the brain's liquid waterbed – followed by the flying shreds of the navy and red silk lining of the hunting cap dispersing everywhere …

Echoing gongs were taking over, heralding the blinding, silent light of death … "Oh, God. Don't look at all my deadly exposed yesterdays … yes … *mea maxima culpa … Pardonnes-moi, mon Dieu … Je t'aime …* I love you …" Uncle Jacques's soul continued his habit of speaking to his God.

* * *

The red mouths of the lady hunt members opened in one voiceless scream.

* * *

The mounted men gasped in horror as they looked down upon the remains of their floundering host's limbs lashing out in uncontrollable spasms as he was thrown spreadeagled, sinking down in the icy incarnadine water.

* * *

The staghounds not already gorging themselves on the dead stag started howling, troubled, as they flocked around their master — licking the blood from the remains of what had been his face in a concerned whimpering lament.

* * *

Il Perfetto finally removed his eye from the socket of his Zeiss scope. Already he felt the knowledge of success draining from him. Success always ended up as failure with him, though the ex-Mafia don had insisted that once Jacques de Lafitte was dead the rest of the de Lafitte family would be easy pickings. Il Perfetto's head throbbed and he felt profoundly sad again. Depression seized him.

"Bloody hell. I've got to stop it. How? How am I ------- well going to help my boy in Kentucky? Blast it, I'm going to get my boy back and nothing is ------- well going to stop me." When his right eye had fully regained its normal balanced vision Il Perfetto knew that earlier he could have taken any other member of the hunt as well as le Comte Jacques. But he never broke his golden rule: one killing at a time. Anyhow, Charles Russell-Lafitte was already spoken for by the ex-don himself later on that same evening in Paris.

Il Perfetto began disassembling his massive rifle but could not stop his thoughts from hounding him again. "I'm fed up with the old man," he thought, "... allowing himself to be seduced out of retirement by his own bastard son. That vile bastard, Il Ciprioni." He felt no joy as he quickly undid and slipped back his Zeiss scope into its small hard leather tube.

His simple delight with having succeeded like in his youth had long disappeared.

Il Perfetto could now only remember – as if it was a long time ago in another age – the fun he'd had as a boy with his brothers. At first they started off from 10 paces: they folded small pieces of square paper that they'd chewed and rolled and folded over the middle of a rubber band which they'd looped around their thumb and trigger finger, and which was held in the shape of a catapult. While still in short trousers they liked firing those paper pellets during their intensive competitions.

Then, as they grew up, they ripped off and hammered the sheets of lead from the broken roof lining of the derelict church in Palermo. They shaped that soft lead about an abandoned wooden tabernacle, then lit endless rows of candles in front of it. The trick was to snuff out the flames from 10 paces by shooting at the wick with an air gun they'd nicked – without touching the candles.

Eventually he'd managed to extinguish a candle every time it was his turn. He could now only vaguely remember the innocence of their joy and their self-confidence: it was great. But he could still recall the injustice he'd felt when his older brother, whom he'd once admired, took just one extra shot. The bastard. He in turn then began to make claims of extra turns from the younger triplets.

Yet he failed to see until this very moment the far greater injustice he'd been perpetrating all these subsequent years, through all the killings he'd carried out throughout his whole damned life. He saw it so clearly now. He knew then he'd rediscovered what he'd sensed so many times before: the reason for that strange cold emptying of himself. Il Perfetto remembered becoming aware of it every time he killed a victim – and the more perfect and demanding the killing the greater the emptiness. Like the feeling he was experiencing at that very moment: engulfed in a state of evil, yet refusing to tackle or even examining the depth of that evil. How could the examining of it have anything to do with the damned dilemma of his hopelessness?

Then he remembered those rare moments when, many years ago, as a boy at Sunday prayers – and even later when was older, when the embers of his conscience caught fire and he heard a voice of total clarity and beauty and authority, speaking: "The seeing eye of grace intruding." His bastard half-brother cleric had mocked at that pure feeling. "The language of heavenly love," the scoffer had scoffed. But he knew.

He knew – in spite of the blasted mockery and the interminable scoffing – that that bastard too must have experienced the truth of that inner voice. It was impossible to stop those powerful assaults. They stole upon him at the most unlikely moments – before or after every killing, or even at the planning stage. Totally damned well unpredictable. "The chaos theory," his half-brother had scoffed. But each time Il Perfetto tried to bury these thoughts, choosing to annihilate them by dismissing them as being incompatible with his trade, they kept on hounding him.

Bloody thoughts like mortal sin. Murder. The $5 million reward money confirmed it as grave matter, if nothing else: the full knowledge of the plans and the full consent of pulling that trigger. He sensed that he would have to choose to condemn his sins, but also that he needed a priest to administer confession, as they called it. Any priest'll do. But not one who'd wants to dominate by looking into his eyes with affected understanding. Priests are the instruments of God and become greater sinners by pretending to be the great forgivers.

They're not available when you want them. An unspoiled cleric is required ... Perhaps a holy monk who understands his role as God's instrument ... Someone who can condemn the evil of sin, yet make allowance for God's love for the damned sinner. But where in God's name was it still possible to find such a priest?

"What you seek is practically impossible with most of us ------- university-educated ones." Il Ciprioni had spoken bitterly when he'd said that. "Most of us find it impossible to regain the simplicity or the humility we've lost. It's nigh impossible for us, the power seekers. The self-important presumptuous lying career bishops already damned – self-condemned to ------- hell." His half-brother had ended with a devilish laugh after he'd spoken, leering with mockery in his voice ... a strange tone to his high pitch. A tone which went beyond screaming – more a high-pitched evil howling.

God, it was weird ... the whites of his eyes growing sombre, his hands becoming darker too ... his face crimson ... the pupils of his eyes burning as if he was already in hell, accompanied by the never-ending bestial high-pitched shrieking of drug-crazed metal music pop idols and their zombie idolaters indulging and hating themselves and each other forever, non-stop, forever ... endless horrific howling.

* * *

The mental image of Ciprioni had vanished as quickly as it had appeared – and Il Perfetto thought again of his escape and of helping his son Il Ragazzo with the Kentucky contract, which was an impossible multiple one. It broke all the family rules. Why had the old man insisted on it? One killing per mission – which the ex-don had never before asked anyone else to break – was the family rule.

Earlier that morning, when Il Perfetto saw the rider whom he'd thought was his son (but had subsequently worked out that it could only have been Charles Russell-Lafitte, the twin of his own adopted son, whom he'd kidnapped 39 years ago), he was happy – just as he'd realised instinctively, similarly aware 12 years ago, at the time of the Oxford contract.

As Il Perfetto's hands swiftly completed the disassembly of his massive sniper rifle he again weighed up the implications of the old man having allowed himself to be seduced out of retirement. He wondered what hold Ciprioni still had over his old man. As he fastened the last buckle of the fishing tackle covering his rifle he knew that ultimately he was only interested in helping his son. With horrid trepidation he felt the family's last-time contract could bestow on his son the curse of a first-time miss. And then he'd never see his boy again.

Il Ragazzo – like Il Perfetto – had never failed to complete a contract in his life, but there was always the dreaded first time. Il Perfetto looked at his watch and his swarthy face began to relax as he calculated the different time zones. He realised that he could still fly to New York then on to Louisville, Kentucky and be in good time (with the replacement of *Concorde*). But after all this time, would his boy be ready to accept his help?

Il Perfetto rapidly untied the thin strip of explosives from around his waist, wrapped them around his fishing pouch, set the timer to go off in a few minutes – and dropped the lot down into the hole of the tunnel. He uprooted two of the 45-degree wooden beams and squeezed out between the sloping stakes.

* * *

The discordant French horn music, muffled by the rising mist, was further shattered by the roar of a four-seater Ferrari flashing through the forest towards Charles de Gaulle airport.

"Yes," Il Ciprioni thought. "He's secured the last seat on Air France's replaced *Concorde* flight to New York. ------- well taken a double risk, using the gold card to book a seat and using the mobile outside the underground bunker. But there was no choice. He had to secure that last ------- seat."

* * *

The heads of the hunt members turned sharply as they heard a dramatic explosion a mile off, coming from the same direction from where they'd thought they'd heard the earlier loud gun shot.

Half an hour later, *Sécurité* helicopters swept their way towards the scene of the tragedy, causing further mayhem in the Lafitte forest.

Chapter Twenty-Three

That same Saturday Charles's vibrant young face, topped by a large mop of hair, broke into a grin as he raced his Bentley flat out. Urged on by his companions, the old motor roared at full throttle down the tree-lined roads converging on central Paris.

Excited by the spinning cyclones of autumn leaves which he stared at in the side mirrors, Charles released his hands from the freshly leather-wrapped steering wheel of his old motor – then gripped it hard again, inhaling its pungent leather smell. He closed his eyes for a moment as the other young singles whooped it up in the back – and it suddenly struck him how irresponsible they were all being, oblivious of what was happening outside their own narrow world.

"Maxim's in 30 minutes," he announced, as the green Bentley screeched to a halt outside the Hôtel de Crillon, overlooking the Place de la Concorde.

"We're going in now without changing," they all shouted.

Charles's crutches were already beside the drivers' door as he hauled himself up on them in his mud-splattered hunting kit. Then he turned, waving, and grinned as Christine – lean as a model (and who had taken the driver's seat) – burned the rubber tyres.

As he swung himself into the lobby of the Hôtel de Crillon he caught sight of his father's manservant sitting on one of the hall chairs. "Hello, Webb. What brings you here?" Webb stood up. His sombre demeanour indicated the importance of the sealed letter, which he handed to Charles.

"Your father was most concerned that I hand you this message in person, Master Charles." As they crossed the marbled hall towards the lifts Charles realised that his father would not send Webb except on some vital mission. He tore open the envelope and took out the letter, just managing to catch the fluttering blue paper slip. The writing on the A4 sheet of paper was in clear capitals:

HUMBURGER IS A TRAITOR. DISCUSS
THIS WITH JACQUES AND CHARLEMAGNE.
TRUST THEM ALONE.

"Strange," Charles thought, as he unfolded the narrowly-folded blue strip. It read:

BE EXTRA CAREFUL, CHARLES.

* * *

The high-speed lift stopped on the third floor. As Webb fumbled with the keys to the door of the family suite Charles reread the short handwritten messages again, wondering what his father had meant when he had underlined the words "Be extra careful, Charles."

He left the notes on one of the bedside tables while Webb helped him strip off his hunting kit. He levered himself up again on to his crutches and swung his head and shoulders underneath the shower, which Webb had already running to the right temperature.

"When did Father give you that note, Webb?" Charles called out. "This morning at the house, Master Charles. He added the folded slip of paper to the envelope after his attempted phone call in the car." Charles heard the concern in Webb's voice. He peered anxiously into the old manservant's eyes as he took the huge blue bath towel from him. "You did well, Webb. Would you care for some tea? Shall I order some? You must be tired."

"No, thank you, Master Charles. But I am a little tired, perhaps."

"Travelling is tiring, Webb. Why don't you take a rest, then see a bit of Paris. Perhaps you can take some of this old luggage back with you tomorrow?

Charles paused for a moment, before saying vaguely, "Is there really any need to continue to hold on to this suite? After all, Anne has her own house in Paris now and Pappa and I hardly need it. I'll discuss it with him when I return from Kentucky."

"Thank you, Master Charles. But I might be needed in Oxford tonight. If it's all right with you, I'll make my way home later on this evening," said Webb.

"Listen," Charles said, pointing to the relentless clattering against the windows, "Hailstones. Here, take my hat and mac, Webb." Charles went to hand them to him but Webb replied, "Thank you, but that won't be necessary, Master Charles."

"No, Webb, I insist." Charles thrust them into Webb's hands. Accepting the hat and mac, Webb was touched. He nodded his head and spoke. "Of course. And thank you, Master Charles." Charles then spotted his new aluminium crutches, which had been hidden underneath the raincoat that had been covering the radiators. "Ah, Webb. Here they are: my first aluminium crutches. Can you take back my wooden ones to Oxford? I'll use the aluminium ones in the States."

Charles picked up his father's note again and tried to ring Uncle Jacques at the chateau, only to hear an out of order tone. Then he dialled the family's trusted confidant Uncle Charlemagne, in Suvretta, Switzerland. Again, he failed to get a connection. With furrowed brow he packed an overnight bag, changed into black tie, and bid Webb farewell before he pressed the button of the lift.

Down in the lobby, he swung himself out of the lift, and noticed the young receptionist waving a fax at him. Her big brown eyes flickered from his floppy hair to his ankles in one involuntary movement. He smiled as he took the fax from her. It read:

> Charles, don't forget my drinks party this evening. It's still on, in spite of the major computer crash in the USA.
>
> Love, Anne. (I've sent this by email too).

Charles grinned, turning to the receptionist. "Which reminds me - could you possibly arrange for my hunting kit to be express-cleaned? It's all upstairs, including my boots. Just ask Webb, our manservant, to get it all together. Could you possibly have it all delivered to my sister's house on the Avenue Foch by this evening?" The receptionist returned Charles's winsome smile. "Certainly, Monsieur Charles."

With that, Charles swung himself across the main lobby, through the entrance door – and into the lashing rain, straight into a waiting taxi. The yellow lights at the Place de la Concorde flickered as they entered the Rue Royale. He tried to collect his thoughts. Why was he still going to Maxim's? That note from his father had changed everything.

When the taxi stopped outside the restaurant the rain had stopped as well. By the time he'd got inside the dark red hall of the restaurant he wished he'd kept his wooden crutches. He missed the warmth of them. Glancing quickly inside the entrance of L'Autobus and right to La Salle he swivelled round – sensing the presence of the old head doorman, who addressed him.

"Bonsoir, Monsieur Charles. Comment allez-vous?"

"Hello, Patrick. Where can I find Christine de Chaumière's party?" The old man smiled knowingly, enlarging his eyes. "Everybody's upstairs in L'Impérial. Come, we've had a new lift fitted," he said, gesturing towards an antique wooden door hiding a modern glass dome.

As Charles floated up to the landing in the glass bubble he saw (through the transparent half door) Christine in the arms of an unusually slender young man. There was something strange about him, and whatever was left of Charles's effusiveness died. His body language reflected the expression on his face as his index finger immediately sought the reverse button for the lift to go back down again. It was just a split second of a glance, but in that instant time seemed to disappear beneath Christine's angry blush as she caught sight of Charles through the glass bubble. Freeing herself from the arms that clung to her she staggered out of the bar, trembling with annoyance.

* * *

Charles was halfway down before he looked back up at her. Instinctively he held his hands up to her. The glass bubble began moving up again, and he felt puzzled about the brittleness of group friendships. He realised then that they knew each other only as an interactive group – as a circle of friends – and not as individual, personal friends. He continued to smile, inviting her into the bubble, holding her wrists as he kissed her cheeks three times. She bit her lip. It was starting to rain again outside.

"I wanted to see you again before leaving Paris," he said.

* * *

She frowned at him, lowering her eyes for an instant, knowing that the right time would present itself for an explanation. "*Charles … je …*"

"Ssh … we'll find something downstairs," he said, smiling, signalling a waiter as they alighted from the lift. "Two dozen oysters, Irish brown bread and the house champagne."

He held her fingers as he admired her perfectly-sculpted beauty. Then he opened his mouth as if he was going to speak, but stopped. He tried again. "Christine," he said, with a sudden seriousness, "It's important. I've seen that chap before." He stopped as he saw her blush with anger.

* * *

"Oh, Charles, he's a nobody." She was still annoyed. "He's just some pushy barrister, always asking questions and always getting everything mixed up. He's a joke in Paris. He's just very persistent and very long-winded." She looked at him with a new sadness. "His name is Jean … Jean Etchips." With that she started to laugh. "He sort of grins and then pounces on girls if they refuse to listen to him." She held up her slim arms, spreading the elegant fingers of her hands and clawing the air. "Once he's got hold of you he won't let go … and because he smells, everyone thinks it's a great joke - which it is, unless one is oneself the victim. We …" She'd started to laugh again. "We've simply started to call him the orang-utang."

"The orang-utang?" Charles queried.

"Have you ever been near one, Charles? Even a baby one? Don't get me wrong. They're sweet – but at a distance, please. You know they have these huge long arms. Anyhow, it was the first time for me today." She nodded her head with emphasis.

"And the last time," Charles interjected, nodding in unison. "He'd just lunged at me as you appeared upstairs on the half landing." They were both laughing now. Charles thumped his chest, gorilla style, making apelike noises: "Ugh, ugh."

Christine joined in, then added, "Charles, he was asking totally inappropriate questions about you and your family and when finally I told him to mind his own business … that was when he lunged at me." She raised her slim arms up again, bending her long slender fingers and expensively-manicured nails into claws, whizzing them in front of Charles's face, and they both fell about laughing once more.

* * *

Once Christine had fled from the upstairs room Jean Etchips dropped his clever buffoonery and found a quiet corner in an adjoining room. He typed out his email on his portable phone and sent it off:

Att. Dr H. Ref. CR-L. Update.

Friends of the Lafitte family are still unaware of assassinations at Eton or in the Lafitte forest. Charles R-L is staying at the Hôtel de Crillon . He intends flying in the family jet to Kentucky tonight. It's raining hard here in Paris and he will be bound to be wearing his yellow mac and his usual black hat. Arrange to kill him as he comes out of the Hôtel de Crillon .

J.E.

* * *

By the time the oyster shells were empty Charles felt relieved that their particular brand of brittle friendship was still intact, but felt disconcerted at having initially jumped to the wrong conclusion. It had been a salutary experience and it taught him to be more circumspect in future. He kissed Christine three times as she pressed the keys of his Bentley into his hand and he swung out of the restaurant. The rain had turned into a thin drizzle so that the streets of the city once more gave off their distinctive Parisian perfume.

Something had changed and yet nothing seemed to have changed. He continued to swing his body between his cold aluminium crutches towards the nearby Automobile Club overlooking the Place de la Concorde, where his Bentley was being admired by a sunburned old man. He was wearing a smart dark grey suit and carrying an old violin case.

Charles looked up at the threatening sky but his thoughts were far away. He was still marvelling at how Annabelle had effortlessly controlled his dancing Arab that morning: the horse would so easily have unnerved a lesser rider. Near the final check, when he was about to ride up closer to Annabelle, Christine had called out excitedly, "Charles, look at those French horns." She'd brought her steaming hunter close to his, pointing her hunting crop towards the distinctive group of hunt servants dressed in their dark blue coats with red collars and green braided lapels … and he'd remembered smiling at the clever girl. Charles then thought how considerate Uncle Jacques was, never hinting that his nephew really ought to abandon his father's old pink coat and wear the proper de Lafitte hunt colours.

"Look, Charles," Christine had called out again. "They have no valves. Isn't it clever, the way they vary the notes simply by moving their bare hands in the hollow bowl of the trumpet?" She had indeed stopped Charles from following Annabelle, but the earlier introduction by Uncle Jacques (however embarrassing at the time) had blossomed into an invitation to spend a weekend with Annabelle at her Scottish family's chateau.

* * *

By the time he reached his Bentley the dark skies had opened up again. The old man with the violin case was nowhere to be seen. He seemed to have vanished into thin air.

Chapter Twenty-Four

B efore sundown that same Saturday, the gilded gates of the gardens and courtyard of Anne's residence were thrown wide open on the Avenue Foch. Guests resplendent in fresh cocktail dresses under bright umbrellas admired the well-trimmed glistening lawns, while others descended briskly from their taxis to the white front door.

Upstairs in the salon the hum of voices mingled with Chopin études. Anne was already in full flow: her intended divorce and remarriage were the centrepiece of the party, with everyone joining in.

"Mark," her voice rang cheerfully, "I'm so glad you're back." She kissed the handsome young man three times, smiling. "How did the voluntary separation go? It's a sweet idea, but isn't rather old-fashioned spending time apart before marriage? But where is my other distant cousin? ... Ah, there you are, Marie dear." Anne touched Marie, and hugged them both together in a great theatrical display. "It is still on, isn't it? she added mischievously, and when Marie kissed her and whispered in her ear, Anne threw her head back, beaming delight. "Thank goodness for that. I would have been terribly cross if it wasn't - I've already spent so much time choosing – and have already bought – my outfit."

She looked around the room with the stylised movement of a young stork trying out its elongated legs and encouraged the handsome Mark de Beaumont to sit down beside his intended, her beautiful distant cousin, Marie St Julien-Lafitte. "Mmm ..." Anne again shared one loud kiss between them both. She looked at them, adding, "I love you both so much," and withdrew, to make more introductions where required.

* * *

One hour later Jean Etchips rang the doorbell, and when René the butler opened the door Etchips pushed roughly passed him with the words, "I'm awfully late, so don't announce me. I'll just slip inside." The old manservant looked puzzled at this fast-talking young man, who was already inside before he could formulate a reply. The butler no longer felt comfortable in this new 21st century and was left stooping sadly in the large chequered hall, staring at the dust on the Gobelins tapestry which hung high over a brightly-polished commode.

* * *

"It was impossible ..." Marie St Julien said hesitatingly to Mark, who was watching Anne reapproach them after she'd done the salon full circle, "... To announce it in time. I mean in its proper form. Those merciless reporters somehow got wind of it first ... and slam ... there it was. I mean, to try to begin to deny it ... really ... Poor Anne."

They rose as their tête-à-tête was interrupted by further introductions. This caused further regroupings as the guests swarmed like butterflies in a hothouse. Soon theatrical greetings were replaced by light conversations which, in the French manner, invited and welcomed interruptions. Among the crossfire of brittle witticisms a small group nodded knowingly at a light-hearted, humorous analysis of the French interpretation of the revised euro monetary policy. The speaker was Mark de Beaumont, the only son of the old Duc Charlemagne de Beaumont, the prominent Swiss banker. All around girls sat vying with each other for attention, pouting, gesturing and prattling ceaselessly, as if the carefully-chosen young men acted as little more than a suitable background for their performance.

"*Ah, oui,* but they do blend in well with the *boiseries,* don't you think? They rather bring the Beauvais tapestries to life." Anne laughed as she encouraged Marie, with some difficulty, to agree with her extravagant conclusions. The two cousins were sitting side by side on a couch in an alcove, while others were sprawled about on huge sofas that had been pulled up closer for intimacy.

Most were by now familiar with the news of Anne's intended divorce, but some were not satisfied with mere confirmation. They wanted more details from the horse's mouth – to be in immediate contact with that touch of tangible conflict, without which life seemed interminably dull. They felt it now, breathed it now, as Anne continued obsessively to run down her marriage. Urged on, Anne tentatively embraced those unexamined freedoms that seemed so tantalising to speculate about ... so wonderfully shocking.

In her mind it seemed as if it was already was all happening, here this instant. Were there no further impending actions? Then why did she feel so uneasy at these shallow attractions? Why, therefore, did she feel frightened at the mere thought of these new freedoms tearing at her marriage vows? Why did she feel, while she almost possessed them, that these freedoms might be illusions? Already they seemed to slink away like snakes in the dark, leaving her frightened. Her shoulders pressed hard into the back of the Louis XIV couch as she sought self-justification through brittle mockery.

She recalled her last conversation with her husband Jean-Pierre in New York. "It's not as if it is me who has been demanding a divorce ... but it is you, through your actions. You are making life impossible for me." She continued recounting her version of their conversation. "My job is as important as yours, but we always end up talking about your promotions."

"But I've had to work so hard to become vice president of the New York branch," had been her version of his reply. "As if that is a justification," she'd said. "Anyway, I told him that all work and no play makes Jean-Pierre a very dull boy, and with that I stormed out and left him sitting on his high and mighty chesterfield in New York."

There was the usual sympathetic laughter, but also a heavy silence. Anne frowned, amazed at listening to the version she herself had selected – with her own possessive voice of freedom urging her on to destroy and erase every former cherished aspiration of her youth … It had been such a splendid wedding at Notre Dame with all her Roman Catholic friends filling up every wicker chair in that exquisite, domed cathedral. Surely everyone had been on her side then? And now? Were they not laughing at her husband with her?

She continued compulsively, violating the very heart of marriage, her breath quickening to short bursts. She changed colour as her heart pumped uncontrollably. Her tongue felt as if it was sinking down her throat. It became thick and dry and yet her destructive hate would out. "… *Ce n'est pas vrai … impossible* …" Encouragement came in floods from all sides. In the ensuing commotion Marie St Julien lightly brushed forward her puffed sleeve to hide the imprint of Anne's nails on her wrist.

"Darling," Marie said in a loud voice, helping up her cousin as she herself jumped up excitedly, speaking in a playful voice, "It completely slipped my mind … Oh … I brought the lace especially from Bruges for you. Come on. It's in the hall – I left it with René. I hope you'll be pleased. Come on." She prattled on purposefully, asking René for a brandy once she was at the edge of the salon.

Then, alone in a bedroom with her cousin, Marie continue to hold Anne's arm. She gently kissed her and asked her to lie down, covering her up with an eiderdown. She leaned over to kiss her again on her hot cheek and whispered to her, "Don't worry, Anne darling. They're already talking about something entirely different. Most people just feel the need to talk: it's just compulsive chatter. The subject is often irrelevant as long as it's exciting. That equates nowadays to destruction. But I love you, darling. Have a short rest. Here, have some more brandy."

"Marie, darling, you are always so kind. Genuinely kind," Anne whispered.

As Marie left the bedroom she wanted to kick herself for not acting more promptly. She was devastated on behalf of her cousin. She saw more clearly than ever that this form of self-flagellation had become an integral part of the distorted and so-called sophisticated 21st-century society.

"The non-acceptance of God's intention for mankind is there for all to see," she thought. Whole new cities, schools and community centres were being built without as much as a chapel. Instead, a need had somehow been created for expensive, perverted amusements and constant new stimuli. The constant renewed search was always for instant and exclusive pleasures, degenerating into hedonism and perversion. Most people knew in the depths of their hearts that these so-called pleasures were incompatible with true happiness. She knew, as most of them did, that they were playing a monstrous game in which each one in turn would some day be a victim. Yet it was considered necessary in Paris, like some sacrificial rite, *contre l'ennui* (boredom).

"In London the 1950s were aptly referred to in a popular song among hoi polloi as, "Putting on the agony, putting on the style; that's what all the young folks are doing all the while". Sadly, the findings of Darwin (a humble God-fearing man in the 19th century in his dogged pursuit of enquiry into a theory of natural selection) became twisted by a menagerie of 20th-century atheistic popularisers of science into the irreverent declaration that "God is dead."

The followers of these sad satanic twisters have now in the present century gone so far as to say that God has become a delusional concept. Even though there is (as was mentioned by her fiancé recently) the helpful reply by that young theologian Thomas Crean, who went to the trouble of writing a specific point by point refutation of those blasphemous claims in his book *A Catholic Replies to Professor Dawkins*. Narrow, straight-line thinking scientists continue to hold on to their scientific views because they cannot understand the spiritual manner of thought of a true theologian. Marie smiled, as she remembered Charles's apt comment, "You can bring horses to water, but you can't make them drink."

* * *

Jean Etchips was waiting for Marie St Julien-Lafitte as she slipped back into the salon. He'd heard so much about this winsome girl and now finally he was in a position to seize the opportunity to interrogate her. He introduced himself as an old friend of the family and, balancing himself on the armrest, invited her to sit down on a nearby armchair. He leaned his small head towards her, talking very quickly, his eyes darting about the room as he flattered the innocent girl. He persisted, sensitive to the girl's emotion only in so far as it served to arouse within him a curious excitement. He praised her exquisite dress. Marie, intrigued by Etchips's flattery, blushed with surprise.

A long way off across the salon Mark saw his fiancée's cheeks flush – and it again struck him how beautiful she always appeared to him, and how he was unworthy of her yet longed to be by her side. Etchips switched his flattery to questioning Marie St Julien about her family's involvement in the de Lafitte Foundation and about her cousin Charles's forthcoming movements. He interspersed his questions with claims about his own latest speaking achievements in the law courts and cast a furtive glance in Mark's direction, not yet aware of their exact relationship.

By now Marie was merely listening to this strange Etchips fellow out of courtesy, finding his legal go-getting exploits and the news of the American computer crash rather repetitive. Puzzled by the lawyer's strange questions (which she instinctively countered with polite deflections) she sought consolation in thinking about Mark instead, and of her fiancé's simple manner and honest nature.

As a student Mark had been recommended by his *Grande Ecole* professor to continue his studies at Oxford and, on receiving brilliant results there, he'd finished with a doctorate at Harvard. For all his intellectual excellence, Mark had remained a very straightforward individual with few pretensions. His life in Geneva and Paris and on his family's country estates was spent in the usual unobtrusive family occupations characteristic of all his close acquaintances.

The one source of sorrow, which Marie was from time to time brutally reminded of by the popular press, was the fatal car accident of Mark's own sister Geneviève. It had affected Mark's boyhood to an extent that Marie was afraid she could never really be fully conscious of. One direct result, Marie discovered, was the development of a philosophy whereby he sought to believe that everyone had to endure hardships – and that these were distributed to each individual relative to their particular circumstances in life, resulting in a broad equality. Somehow she'd felt at home with that, and loved him for it.

Marie too realised that she had always led a sheltered life. Who did she know, other than those she had been introduced to by her family or very close friends ... or those kind helpers who devoted one or two weeks of their own holidays every year to the disabled in Lourdes? Over the years they had become her friends, together with many of those pilgrims whom she had also grown to love during those intimate days of caring. Her soft brown eyes glowed with kindness as an image of Betty, the cleaning lady from one of the Oxford colleges whom she'd helped make up the beds with in one of the hospitals in Lourdes last summer, sprang to mind. "Such wit," she thought.

While she automatically deflected the flood of extraordinary personal questions put to her by Etchips she smiled at this total stranger, who was still talking non-stop. He was so inquisitive, so extraordinarily different from most of her friends, so she closed the encounter with a laugh. "I really do talk too much about myself. Let's talk about you, shall we?"

"Aha. That's one thing, Marie, that I never do with my friends." Coming from someone else Marie might have found this amusing, but she suddenly found that she really did not wish to prolong her conversation with this tiresome fellow. Etchips concluded that this type of girl was too self-assured – and also that she, as a potential source of information about the Lafitte family, was far too discreet.

Already on his feet, he said, "Let me get you a drink." With that he disappeared out of the salon. He opened the front door of the empty hall himself, stepped out into the dark glistening drizzle and ran back to his car at the entrance to the tall gates. There he made out his report and emailed it off on his mobile to Geneva. He waited for a reply. And waited.

Chapter Twenty-Five

W hen Webb surveyed the family's rooms at the Hôtel de Crillon it was already getting dark that Saturday evening. He decided everything had been properly packed and that the rooms were empty and tidy. "As they ought to be," he thought. He closed the windows securely against the constant drizzle. Then he thought he'd better try to telephone Sir Basil again. When there was no reply on his direct line he rang the receptionist.

"The telephone doesn't seem to be working, Miss. Could I possibly ask you to try, please?" Webb persisted with the telephonist. "It's important," he said.

"*Ne quittez pas. Zut alors*, the line is dead, Monsieur."

Webb was taken aback by the curtness of her reply, but was reminded of Sir Basil's comment about the French language. He blamed himself, as well for being unnecessarily concerned at not being able to get through to Oxford. Having lost every single member of his own family during the great war while serving as batman to Sir Basil, he'd grown used to all his master's little ways. He'd even learned to cope with all the other eccentricities of an Oxford don after he'd entered service at the family house overlooking Oxford.

Over many years he'd become happy in the Russell-Lafitte house and felt himself to have become an indispensable part of the family. After the early and sudden death of Lady Russell-Lafitte in childbirth he'd witnessed and participated in all the activities of the children growing up. He had shared the joys and the occasional sadness of the family, and somehow he felt to be a useful and loving part of them. As he slipped on Charles's yellow mac and black trilby the thought struck him that Charles possessed the same qualities of courtesy and kindness of Sir Basil, his master. With that he pulled the door of the suite firmly shut behind him, and placed two very heavy suitcases into the lift. He was still concerned about not getting through to Oxford on his way down, but he resolved to try again at the airport.

As the lift doors slid open in the lobby the newly-appointed young assistant evening porter sprang forward in Webb's direction. As he passed by the porter's lodge again he picked up a huge multicoloured hotel golfing umbrella from behind his desk. The young lad opened it up, inviting Webb (wearing Charles's black hat and yellow gabardine) to take shelter from the downpour before approaching the taxi waiting outside. The young porter wheeled the two heavy suitcases over the exit in the buggy and made a great display of loading them one by one into the back of the waiting Citroën taxi to the left of the front door.

As the drizzle continued to lash down it could be seen that – curiously for a wet evening – one of the unlit windows on the other side of the street was ajar, with an edge of net curtain hanging out limply in the rain. Nobody could have seen the high-powered rifle resting on the back of a plain wooden chair. The butt of the rifle, with a silencer and telescopic sight secured on top, was cradled against the shoulders of the well-dressed old man sitting upright on a similar chair. The open violin case was lying beside him.

The young porter stood to attention beside the rain-splashed taxi and waited as he proudly held up the brightly-coloured golfing umbrella. After an awkward pause it began to dawn on Webb what was expected of him. He jabbed both his hands into the pockets of the yellow gabardine, searching for a tip, as the Parisian rain continued to drum wet music on the open parasol.

The ex-Mafia don had been alerted by the hotel's bright umbrella, and immediately thought he'd recognised the distinctive yellow gabardine with the black trilby he'd been told to look out for. His view of the victim's face was partially unclear. "Seize the moment" had always been his advice to his sons. Just as the ex-don was about to pull the trigger, the young lad – aware that he was about to receive his tip – bent forward, robot-like, to open the door of the taxi. The orange light from inside the taxi did not give the ex-Mafia don a clearer view of his victim, but the light shining on the top of the broad lapels of the yellow raincoat and on the nondescript human face underneath the black hat were positive proof that this was certainly his victim. The ex-don, tired of waiting – and excusing his own age – ignored the advice he'd always given his grown-up sons and pulled the trigger.

* * *

Webb, with his hands still inside the pockets of the yellow mackintosh, was flung right back against the limestone wall of the hotel. The bullet left only a small hole in the front of the yellow gabardine but exited in a splash of blood, having churned up Webb's heart. Webb's lean rheumatic fingers automatically closed around a Lourdes rosary in the gabardine pocket as he slid down the blood-splattered wall, leaving a dark streak of blood on the damp limestone. Webb's nostrils filled with the unmistakable smell of rain from the wet Parisian pavements. His smarting eyes, clenched shut in agony, seemed to see painful misty images of his five brothers falling on the beach of a war-torn Normandy as they were gunned down in the pelting rain. His rosary-entangled hand had jerked itself out of the yellow mac and he managed to touch his forehead, with the words of the Lord's Prayer on his lips.

The assassin's second bullet tore the beads from the servant's pale fingers. Webb's dazed eyes were lifeless as he lay in the drenched yellow mackintosh while he oozed blood on to the pavement beside a crumpled black trilby:

Yellow and black and pale and hectic red.

The words of one of Sir Basil's favourite poets would honour poor Webb in that fatal Parisian scene.

* * *

The ex-don closed his violin case and was already looking up the code for Geneva. He started dialling the number to announce the death of Charles Russell-Lafitte to Dr Humburger.

Chapter Twenty-Six

A nne Russell-Lafitte slipped back into the salon after her short rest and looked around with renewed confidence. She touched Mark's arm as he crossed the salon. "Mark, you and Marie are booked to fly with Charles to Kentucky next week. By the way, where is my brother and darling Marie?" Turning to address her cousin who was just joining them, she said, "Marie darling, thank you. You've been so kind." Anne kissed her cousin and started again. "Did you know that you've both been invited to George's Kentucky hunt ball next Saturday? Charles will fly you there. He's going too, as he wants to test out his new jet. George also wants you to stay on for his special lawn meet the next day. It's known as George's Sunday."

Marie flushed pink at the joy of spending more time with her fiancé. Mark gently squeezed her hand and Marie beamed. "Good. That's settled." Anne kissed her cousins, saying, "Charles will be so pleased you're both going with him."

Just then — seeing Charles with his aluminium crutches entering the salon from across the far side of the room — she waved to him, saying to her cousins, "I'll arrange for him to pick you up later next week, after you've sorted out your kit." Anne continued to signal to her brother as she crossed the salon. She whispered goodbye to her other guests, who were now drifting out in twos and threes, before welcoming Charles with outstretched arms.

"I'm so glad that you finally arrived, Charles," she admonished him, whispering in his ear as they embraced. "You seem changed - much more handsome, of course. Your reading of theology at Oxford must agree with you. How is my darling Rupy? Did Uncle Jacques find a good fresh stag this morning?"

"Darling Anne, Rupert is on the mend and I rather suspect he persuaded Papa to take him to the wall game this morning. Hasn't Uncle Jacques arrived yet?" Charles asked.

"Dearest Rupy. I must give him a ring later." Anne blushed at her negligence. She embraced Charles again then held him at arm's length, looking him up and down, indulging that extraordinary feeling of possessiveness peculiar to brother and sister.

"I like your new outfit," Charles laughed. She kissed his cheek again and then turned herself around to show off her new chiffon dress. It was the colour of a multitude of wild flowers, anemones and poppies, set off with white and green looped multicoloured streamers tied high around her neck. She turned proudly around again, freely wafting the streamers. She clasped her hands loosely around his waist again with the words, "You're right, you know: it's the country look." She looked up at him. Delight streamed from her tanned face.

"Where is Uncle Jacques? I was expecting him. I suppose he's been delayed taking on yet more responsibilities. D'you remember? Pappa used to always say, "If you want something done quickly ask the busiest person first and he'll do it." As she escorted Charles to an alcove in between more goodbyes, it occurred to her how much she herself had changed. She lowered her eyes, pleased that she was now in a position to control the anxieties of the past month even if only for a brief moment now that her brother was here. She indulged herself, allowing herself to participate in the wonderful fresh normality of family bonding. "Doesn't anyone ever wonder why you're not married yet, Charles?" Her younger brother laughed. "Everyone's given me up as a lost cause: father's footsteps and all that."

By the time the butler finally cleared away the glasses and brought in some freshly-made coffee Anne's naturally flippant manner had returned. She sat down gesticulating wildly. "So like Mildred. You know what I mean, swishing her arms about like this … Oops." Anne's hand had whacked René's tray, but he had somehow managed to avoid spilling the coffee over the Aubusson carpet. "René, have I done something ghastly?" Anne smiled winsomely, and then continued, unperturbed. "Yes. Fancy calling the Greek ambassador 'My little revolutionary.' I mean to say, Charles, it's not as if the poor man could have been completely insensitive to it. Fancy."

Charles sat frowning. Suddenly Anne again wanted to know, "Seriously, Charles, why aren't you married yet?"

"Anne, if you weren't my sister and not already married, I should propose right now."

"Oh, do … and I accept."

"Her voice rang throughout the near-empty drawing room. She leapt up, dragging him with her towards the French windows, which overlooked the rain-sodden terrace. "I accept. I accept."

"Anne, which is it to be? Me or the Moët & Chandon?"

"That's not fair," she said. And she sat down again, pleased at having shown him without any inhibition the healthy frivolous side of her nature that had been so absent from her life during the past few months.

But Charles was frowning again now. "Charles, what?"

"Anne, darling," he whispered, taking both her hands in his. "I know it is considered chic in these crazy times for a wife to be thought of as being free and independent of her husband, but surely this is contradictory? Surely one gets married because one wants to become one with the other and needs the other to be at one with one's new, ever-evolving self?"

"Charles, I know all that, but in practice this is so, so difficult. *Et Jean-Pierre est vraiment …*"

"*Impossible,*" he interjected in French, amused at their ability to read each other's thoughts in either language. "*Non,* he is so vain." Anne flushed crimson as she stressed that last word. Charles continued to look at his sister fondly, his eyebrows twitching as he puzzled to find the words … and he ended up frowning. "Anne darling, I know Jean-Pierre loves you. He loves you so much." The intensity of his expression had an immediate effect on Anne's blue eyes, which were now moist. She sought his downcast face and with her right hand gently pushed back the hair on his high forehead until his dark deep-set eyes met hers. She couldn't bear the honesty of his expression, and she embraced him.

He said to her, "Hating is wanting the other person to not exist, and you aren't capable of that, Anne" he whispered it again in a broken voice. "I know Jean-Pierre would so welcome a warm hug. You were such good friends. He feels the end of a marriage – anyone's marriage, no matter who's to blame – as the ultimate failure. He wants a reconciliation. And you must start it, Anne. You alone are capable of it."

"Charles, no. No. I just can't," Anne said.

"Do it for Father," Charles said. "He doesn't care." Anne said this with a coldness that startled Charles. "Anne, that is unworthy of you … and it's also not true. Absolutely not true. He … he cares dreadfully. He really does care, awfully."

Anne winced at the intensity of Charles's emotion. She looked at him warmly and felt caught by this sudden re-emergence of heartfelt truth, aware that she herself (deep down) had known this all the while. Her blue eyes flashed with annoyance at herself, and she turned her solemn face towards the tall French windows. She rose from her seat as the tears in her eyes threatened to roll down and destroy her expensively-powdered face. Her lips moved but she did not speak.

The silence froze, and then a greater stillness possessed her. She heard Charles swallowing loudly, and heard him speak her name again. "Anne?" It sounded like the bell that used to toll on the hour in Grandfather's Biarritz chateau, where they had sometimes spent their childhood holidays. Anne continued staring out of the window into the sombre evening sky and listened to the rain tapping on the window. "Who am I?" she thought, "And what has happened?" her inner voice demanded.

Then she jerked her head round and looked at her brother. Her eyes were crystal-clear now. She smiled brilliantly at him and, as she sat down again – embracing Charles for his honesty – goodness streamed from her, but she remained silent. Charles squeezed her shoulder. "Anne, Jean-Pierre will be arriving in Oxford tomorrow morning and has begged you to lunch with him at Brown's. My best friend's a Benedictine abbot – and he told me recently that, looked at positively, obedience is the easiest thing in the world."

"Charles, you know very well that it's not easy. You know Uncle Jacques wants you to become his successor – and so does Pappa, and yet you don't seem to be prepared to do anything about it."

"An invitation is different from a marriage vow," he replied with a broad grin. "And, as it happens, in the light of my meeting this morning with Uncle Jacques, I may indeed chuck in my new degree and see how I can help the family. But I'll only decide after I've spoken to Pappa again. What do you recommend I should do?"

The unexpected switch from her own dilemma to his jolted her. It helped her to see her own predicament in a new light. Suddenly everything seemed so different, and her smile went to her intelligent eyes. Instantly she translated his personal question to a serious commitment as she bravely held out her hand. "I will if you will."

"Done." Charles squeezed her hand and they embraced again as he replied, "I'm so pleased, Anne. I promised to phone Jean-Pierre in New York. Shall I tell him the good news? No. You do it, and then you can make all the arrangements yourselves for lunch ..." He stopped for a moment. "Of course this eastern seaboard problem won't let us get through."

"I'm so nervous, Charles. Could you possibly make the arrangements with Jean-Pierre? I've got to start packing. Send him my love ... and Charles ... Thank you." She gave him a kiss on his left cheek then stood up and left to go to her room, calling for René. Charles immediately picked up the telephone, but it was dead. He tried again, then he remembered he might be able to overcome the software malfunction using the latest communication technology via LA on board the new jet.

René arrived discreetly, showing Charles the brown paper parcel which had just arrived with the words, "For you, Monsieur Charles."

"Ah, my hunting kit. Squeeze it into my bag in the hall, René. By the way, could you report to France Télécom that your line is still out of order?"

* * *

Anne bounced back again. "Mark and Marie really do suit each other, don't they, Charles? Oh ... and make sure you meet up with our distant cousin next Saturday in Kentucky. Her name, by the way, is Dr Caroline."

"Matchmaker … I've just tried to speak to Jean-Pierre. Did you know this line is out of order? I've just told René to report it but I'll try to talk to Jean-Pierre from the jet via LA."

"Thanks, Charles. By the way, I told Mark and Marie you're collecting them next week. They're flying with you to George's ball next Saturday. I should have told you earlier. George did insist on all of you coming before I left New York."

She suddenly frowned, before adding, "There was an odd little man at my party, earlier - a gatecrasher. What's his name? Jean something or other? Anyhow, we call him the orang-utang. I saw he was badgering poor Marie, trying to get information about the family. He's been noticed recently hanging around our crowd, asking intrusive questions and no doubt coming to false conclusions."

"Don't worry, Anne. I caught a glimpse of him earlier today. Forget him. I'm off to Scotland for a few days, but will be back to collect Marie and Mark next Saturday for George's Kentucky weekend."

Charles made little of his earlier concern for Anne's sake, allowing her to feel relaxed. He felt relieved when she replied, "Want any books from Blackwell's, Charles?"

"Yes, there is one, actually: the new Oxford Dictionary of Theology."

"But you said you were giving it up."

"Exams, yes … but not my love of the subject. Bye, darling."

Chapter Twenty-Seven

"Jean-Pierre, we've a poor line … What's that again?" Anne pressed her mobile phone to her ear in Oxford that Sunday and replied, "I'll try too, darling." She listened as he told her he loved her and that he'd just landed at Heathrow, but was she safe in Oxford?

"Well I'm glad you've landed at Heathrow. You're not actually saying Oxford's unsafe? Don't be silly, darling. It's just that Pappa and Rupy aren't back yet. I'm just worried for them. Even Webb, who's always absolutely reliable, seems to have been delayed in Paris. I'm glad we can use our mobile. Our house telephone line still hasn't been fixed yet."

Anne shivered in the unheated room off the main hall of her father's house. She continued to listen to Jean-Pierre, then replied, "What a good idea. Yes, Blackwell's bookshop is open now on Sundays. Yes, I'll meet your tutor - er, MI6 friend - later at Brown's. I didn't catch that … Right, I'll tell Nanny. I'll call back this afternoon. Hopefully Rupy and Papa will be back by then. Bye, darling. In the meantime, I'll see you at 12.30."

Anne ran back upstairs to say goodbye to Nanny and then went out quickly to apologise to the London taxi driver whom she had kept waiting at front of the house. Slipping into the back seat of the cab, she asked the driver to go to the famous bookshop on Broad Street. She was relieved that Jean-Pierre had managed to reach her on her mobile. She said a quick prayer in gratitude. A return to normality? Hopefully.

The avenue curved smoothly as they motored from the house. Anne turned sadly around in the taxi. She loved the family house back in its own unique world in Oxford, and never liked to leave its manicured lawns. Curiously, as soon as she heard the rattle caused by the taxi crossing the cattle grid she began to feel like a frightened schoolchild again. Where were Pappa and Rupert?

* * *

Il Terzina, once he'd heard and caught a glimpse of the black London cab entering the gate earlier that Sunday morning, was now acting as a lookout for his other triplet and was waiting in his hired green van opposite the main gate of the house.

As he heard the taxi coming back down the avenue and watched it clatter over the cattle grid he raised his small binoculars. There was an attractive, worried-looking young lady wearing a Hermès scarf at the back of the cab who was constantly glancing back as she went through the main gates.

"This is something else and no ------- mistake," he said in peasant Italian, checking the well-thumbed photographs beside him. Nevertheless, there was no doubt in his mind that the girl in the cab was the Russell-Lafitte girl on his list. He started his engine and tried to get his triplet on his mobile. He followed the black taxi down Headington Hill towards the plain, and over Magdalen Bridge.

At the entrance to Oxford High Street the taxi turned right, down Long Walk. "Why is my brother not answering his mobile?" he thought. They were already past Rhodes House, turning left towards Wadham College, and stopped only at the traffic lights at the King's Arms. He was right behind the taxi now, and could see the back of the victim's head covered by the distinctive colourful Hermès scarf very clearly. The taxi turned right and stopped outside the Sheldonian Theatre, opposite Blackwell's bookshop.

Il Terzina shouted down his mobile, "Ah, it's you. Yes, I'm sure it's her. She's stepping out of the taxi now ... wait ... she's going straight into Blackwell's bookshop." He remained silent as he received instructions, then complained, "OK, but I'll have to drive around. It's double yellow lines all around here now and the traffic wardens are out in force. Yes, I know it's because it's Sunday." After half an hour of idling in front of the Sheldonian, which allowed him to keep an eye on Blackwell's, Il Terzina checked his watch and swore out loud, "What the bloody hell's keeping my younger brother?"

He glanced into the rear-view mirror and to the side and the front of the green van – and then he saw his brother in the distance coming towards him, dressed for all the world like a well-tanned tourist in winter. He was holding a large, partially-unfolded map and an umbrella in his left hand: a camera was hanging from his neck and on his back was an elongated khaki-coloured rucksack, with the semblance of a squash racket handle sticking out of it. As the tourist walked alongside the green van he tapped the driver's window with his umbrella. He pointed to his map and bent down, pretending to ask for directions.

Il Terzina had now lowered his window and showed his triplet the photographs, pointing to Blackwell's. "She's all yours now. I'll meet you at that pub sometime after lunch." He indicated to the King's Arms at the corner and drove off to find a parking spot for his van. Il Terzina's youngest brother crossed Broad Street and waited between the two blue doors of Blackwell's bookshop, pretending to admire the display of the latest local bestsellers through the window.

He spotted his intended victim through the glass frontage. He could see from her wild exaggerated gestures that she had just recognised someone. "How do these ------- people live?" he thought. Both girls were obviously recalling something. He looked at his watch. It was approaching noon. "The bells will start to ring out soon," he thought as he continued to watch the two girls, and he could see that she was clearly persuading her friend to join her. He would really have to play it by ear now.

"Good. She's plainly failed to persuade her. What a stroke of ------- luck. We have invested too much time and money into this project," he thought. Anyhow, he'd won the toss against his other triplets and he was not going to fail now. It was an extra fee and it was a big one. "We've always split it evenly," he thought, but he wanted it to be a surprise, because he was the baby triplet, younger by just five minutes. "It's not the money, but it's still competition," he thought, and relaxed again as he thought of Christmas. "Whatever happens, it'll be a real feast this year."

* * *

Suddenly Anne burst through the right blue door, laden with Blackwell's carrier bags. Il Terzina could have touched her: he inhaled the Givenchy III perfume that followed her, floating in the air. "She's beautiful in an expensive sort of way, I suppose," he thought cynically as she walked passed him, and he followed her from a suitable distance. She was in a hurry and, as she cast a glance through the railings of Trinity College, she ignored the scruffy buildings of the now blatantly left-wing Balliol College. Then she turned right, crossed St Giles at the Martyrs' Memorial and walked straight into The Randolph Hotel in Beaumont Street.

* * *

Il Terzina was unhappy with the two exits from the hotel and quickly looked towards the main frontage to the Ashmolean Museum. "But that's ------- well too exposed. It's ------- well freezing, sitting on these ------- memorial steps," he thought, but it was the only vantage point which gave him total visibility of both exits. The perfect tourist, Il Terzina pretended to study the Oxford map again.

Having left her bags with the hall porter and powdered her nose, it was 12.15 before Anne reappeared. She crossed Beaumont Street, walked up St Giles past the Taylor Institution. She walked past Blackfriars and tried to enter St Benet's Hall. The door was locked, however and – not remembering the combination – she continued walking along the Woodstock Road. She checked her watch as she gazed longingly at the patisseries displayed in the window of Maison Blanc.

Anne hurried past Brown's restaurant and went inside St Aloysius church, which the Oratorians had resurrected from a state of near abandon by the Jesuits. "Had they not once been proud to be known as the Soldiers of Christ?" she thought. Sadly, they had temporarily descended into becoming latter-day secular social workers. No doubt a new leader in the future would bring back Jesus at its central focus, as it was (after all) called The Society of Jesus.

The St Philip Neri fathers (the Oratorians) on the other hand – with the zeal of balanced religious dedication – continued to focus on the nobility of Jesus the Son of God through prayer and hard work. Had they not already converted this large ineffective church into a vibrant parish church of daily worship? Jean-Pierre had told her about John Henry Newman, the renowned Anglican scholar from Oxford University, who in the 19th century had become a leading light of the Oxford Movement – his attempt to refocus Anglicanism back to the basics of Christian worship through ardent prayer, self-sacrifice and honest scholarship. Newman, an ardent Anglican, was clearly guided by the Holy Spirit and, after many years of hard work and prayer, concluded and accepted that it was more probable that Roman Catholicism was more likely than any other religion to be the one true church founded by Jesus Christ.

Anne looked around the recently-refurbished church where Newman had himself once preached as the founder of the Oratorians in the UK, and smiled when she saw an elegant portrait of the cardinal in a gold frame. Recently he'd been beatified by Pope Benedict XV1 and Jean-Pierre had a long time ago suggested to Anne that Newman, now on his way to being declared a saint by the Roman Catholic church, should have a fitting chapel in this same church dedicated to this forthcoming Oxford saint.

After a few minutes of intensive prayer to John Henry – and for her son Rupert, her husband Jean-Pierre and her brother Charles – Anne came out, turned right with determination and without further hesitation retraced her steps back to Brown's restaurant.

* * *

Il Terzina – who had followed his victim from a distance, and had thought he'd lost sight of her – now rediscovered her striding towards Brown's restaurant. He kept a keen eye on Anne's movements and crossed the Woodstock Road at the traffic lights facing Brown's, then stopped and started to set up his camera on its tripod at the edge of Woodstock Road beside Stella Mannering's interior design studio.

There he stood, taking pictures like a regular tourist hanging around for a good photographic shot. His whole life consisted of waiting, hiding, watching, feigning – all so that he might eventually get just one better killer shot.

He liked shooting. He and his triplets were good at shooting. And after this one there was just one more assignment in Ireland. Il Terzina pretended to take more photographs of Anne sitting in the triple window at Brown's with his long-lens camera, giving him the perfect opportunity of keeping an eye on his victim. He watched her raise her hand with three fingers raised to one of the apron-wearing waiters, who went to fetch a newspaper, while Anne waited for her guests to arrive.

He looked at his watch. It was 12.25 hours. Yes … a table for three meant there'd be two more for lunch. "From which I'll take care of one, perhaps even two today," he thought.

Chapter Twenty-Eight

When he'd left Paris and arrived in Edinburgh the previous Saturday night Charles had already – using the cockpit's latest digital communication's technology via LA – spoken to Jean-Pierre in New York from the new jet's pilot's cabin.

"Good. What? Yes, we've heard," replied Charles, in a cool voice. "Goodness me. Not expected to be repaired before Sunday night next week? Yes, I've just come from Anne's. She'll try if you will. Yes, isn't it? She'd love to have lunch with you at Brown's, 12.30, next Sunday. She sends her love. Yes, Brown's on the Woodstock Road. Yes. At 12.30 next week. Give her a ring at home in Oxford on your mobile when you get to Heathrow. Bye." With that he went straight to his club, so that he could manage a few hours' sleep before driving off before daybreak for Coolin Castle, in the Highlands.

After a tour de force of driving Charles arrived in Kinlochewe, Western Ross, high up in the Northern Scottish Highlands late on Sunday morning.

"Hello? Can I speak to Annabelle Beauchamp, please?"

"Who shall I say is speaking?" asked the houseboy at Coolin Castle, near Kinlochewe.

"Charles Russell-Lafitte here."

"Hold the line, please." There was a long silence, then the slow hazy voice of Annabelle. "Hello, Charles. How nice of you to call. Where are you?"

"Annabelle, how are you? I'm off to church in your local village, so don't expect me until around 12.30. Is that frightfully late?"

"That's perfect. We don't normally have Sunday lunch till one. See you then."

Charles left his specially-fitted UK Bentley near the telephone kiosk, and made his way through the frosty air of the tiny Scottish village along its wide street to the rebuilt tiny Gothic Catholic chapel. Once inside, a deeper calm came over him. One by one some of the villagers traipsed up the narrow aisles. By the time the sermon was under way the small chapel was actually warm.

"How then is one to measure one's life's work?" asked the preacher. For him, a giant of a man, it was an important question. It seemed at first – as he turned to leave the pulpit – that he was going to leave it hanging in the air. But then stopped, turned back to the congregation and, whispering loudly, he said, "Not only now, but at frequent intervals, should we not weigh up our efforts on our own scales of conscience?" The pastor closed his eyes, which was the sign for his flock to join him in prayer.

"Teach me, O Lord, to be generous; to give and not to count the cost; to fight and not to heed the wounds; to labour and not to seek reward save that I know that I do thy Holy Will." The gentle giant opened his eyes again and whispered, "And if ... in those moments of failing when we have let you down, O Lord ... and when we think of you yet somehow persist in our failings ... let us not, because of our weakness, despair." In a gentle voice he added, "Remember always: God is infinitely merciful."

His massive head shuddered as he struck his breast repeatedly – and his voice vibrated with massive volume as he lit up with emotion, personalising the communal sentiment, "*Mea culpa, mea culpa, mea maxima culpa.*"

Then his voice dropped a tone; a deeper sadness crept into his earthy voice as he continued, "Why do we criticise the religions of different nations and peoples? This ridiculous pettiness is not helpful. Are we not all one in acknowledging the great beauty, magnificence and omnipotence of one God, Father, Son and Holy Spirit, Creator of Heaven and Earth? Why then, must pride persuade us to be different? You, the congregations, do not want division – and it is you who must pray for us, for a more humble clergy, especially theologians, to serve you better. Is that not so?"

He left the question in mid air, and slowly the big humble giant walked down the pulpit steps. He stopped halfway down, turning to look at them. "Aye? Of course, worst of all are the vainglorious types among us who end up dismissing God altogether – who instead seek to propose scientific theories, thereby reducing the freedom of us all … so that their atheistic secular solutions can horrifically comply with their narrow sad dull terms of so-called scientific logic. Some of you have witnessed the beauty of Oxford, but have you not also been affronted by those recent horrible scientific buildings? Do we really want to be influenced by their type of mindlessness?" The big man then blessed himself slowly.

"No. We are all heirs to the Kingdom of Heaven as sons and daughters of God with a free spirit. That free spirit is like his spirit: totally free … God-given. We, each one of us, must learn to cherish it more. It is God-given."

Lifting his bushy eyebrows again, he made his way back to the altar. Before the offering of the Eucharist he whispered loudly again, "This is the moment when Christ becomes truly present again – as he promised at his Last Supper – in the guise of bread and wine. Transubstantiation is the very heart of Mass. It's as close as we'll ever get to Christ in this world."

The elevation of the host and chalice was accompanied with the universal reverence of sacred prayers and the ringing of bells in homage, familiar to billions of Catholics throughout the world. After helping with the distribution of communion to the congregation the young sacristan soon went to the back of the organ to activate the hand-operated air pump, squeezing out the congregation's final familiar hymn. This was the clue for some of the men who were huddled at the back of the chapel to make for the exit.

* * *

Driving through Glen Carron along the banks of the lake, which reflected the snow-capped peaks of Beinn Alligin, Charles marvelled at the expanse of the deserted moors and mountains. Coming out of a turn in the road he spotted a cluster of 17th-century turrets, which he'd been told to look out for. They vanished as he drove up the endless pinewood avenue, then again the granite castle suddenly reappeared at close quarters.

Large, immaculately-kept lawns surrounded the neat ivy-clad building. The massive hall door was slowly drawn open and a prim houseboy in a standard kilt beckoned him in, before hurrying off to announce his arrival. Inside, lining the granite stone hall, were many clocks, stag's antlers, stuffed eagles and foxes in glass cages. A massive array of dull armour plate was just visible, higher up in the reaches of the monumental walls.

In the blazer-red library, adjoining the bright yellow dining room, Annabelle sat astride a green leather-upholstered club fender in front of a roaring wooden fire. She continued stroking her black retriever. She'd decided not to change, and still wore the hacking jacket and yellow jodhpurs from her early-morning ride.

Her mother was reading the Sunday papers sitting on one of the two great chintz covered sofas that faced each other on either side and were set back some distance from the large marble mantelpiece. As the hall boy announced the arrival of Charles Russell-Lafitte, she put down the article about progress in China she was reading and looked at her daughter and sighed quietly. "I think perhaps you might have changed, Annabelle," she said, with a sweet yet serious smile, unsure of what was best for her daughter (whom she loved and had tried hard over the years not to spoil). With that she cast a cursory glance at the newspapers that lay scattered about her on the sofa.

Annabelle stood up, away from the blaze. Feeling her cheeks burn she glanced at the large gilt mirror edged with stiffies and started to remove her tweed jacket, revealing a tight-fitting navy ribbed pullover. She blushed as her father welcomed Charles into the room. Proud of her slim figure, she turned towards slowly her guest.

"Did you have difficulty in finding us, Charles? We are rather inaccessible," she laughed. "I did warn you, didn't I?" she said. Stepping forward from the club fender and mantelpiece she touched his hand but did not offer him her cheeks for a kiss, as she might have done in France.

"Here, Charles. Do have some Croft's Original." Sir Jeremy pressed a sherry glass into Charles's hand before starting on a detailed history of the region. Only when the many clocks in the entrance hall chimed one o'clock was Sir Jeremy reminded that he'd been hogging the conversation again. Lady Alexandra smiled, looking sweetly at her husband then at Charles and her daughter. Then she looked into space, not daring to indulge further the happiness she felt for her daughter. "He truly is such a handsome fellow," she thought to herself, and she hoped her sweet Annabelle might find happiness at last. They strolled into the dining room, all chattering at once.

"Bless this food, dear Jesus, and all present." The houseboy and parlourmaid stood to attention during the prayers before meals. At one end of the table Charles briefly and quietly brought Sir Jeremy up to date about the discussions he'd had with Uncle Charlemagne and the role Interpol was now playing. Suddenly Charles turned towards Lady Beauchamp as if he'd forgotten something.

"Your sister made me promise to pass on her love."

"Sweet of you to have remembered," she replied. "We are very close." She smiled sweetly. As the houseboy arrived with the large silver salver of game, Sir Jeremy spoke up. "Cook has done the grouse and ptarmigan proud, Charles. I shot them myself last week. I think it's just the end of the season."

* * *

After coffee Charles and Annabelle set off in his adapted Bentley. "A twin of the one available in Paris," Charles hinted as he drove through the snow-covered hills that circled the lochs. She continued to indulge their comfortable chatter, feeling inexplicably happy, driving with her childhood hero – whose attention she was now, unaccountably again – trying so hard to resist.

Suddenly the appearance of the sun's rays brought out what remained of the multicoloured gorse, rushes and scrub verge. She felt pleased that the vast expanse of countryside, so remote, was such a comfort to her – just as it had always been in her childhood. How relaxed things were then. The holidays in Switzerland with her relations and friends, her visits to the warm Italian cities – it had all been so natural then, so acceptable ... so very much even the expected thing.

Now there would need to be a reason. A why? … an accomplishment. Her simple country confidence was continually assaulted by questions. She blushed even now at the memory of her recent embarrassment in the common room at Wolfson, when she'd been asked what job she had actually been doing during the summer months. It had made her feel that she had to invent one in order not to offend the other graduates. The natural joy of calm leisure had been replaced by the kicks everyone now craved for – the mass highly-organised speed holidays, with their obligatorily required adrenalin buzz. But her face lit up as they approached the small village of Kinlochewe at the head of Loch Maree, under the peaks of the Beinn Eighe mountains.

She put her hand on his arm for an instant to signal to him to drive more slowly along the edge of the Loch, where gnarled oaks like fantastic monsters acted as a hedge to the snow-clad peaks. Clouds began to form, hiding the rays of the sun again. The moorland, sombre now, caused her eyes to switch back to the edges of the loch, which had acquired the dark green and purplish colours.

"Do let's drive down to Plockton," she prompted. "Take the second left." Derelict stone cottages, forlorn against the barren mountains, added to the eerie silence of the Highlands. The deserted yacht club of Plockton where, as a young girl, she had sailed in summer seemed so changed, she reflected. It was a skeleton of its former self, with just a few neglected dinghies, half frozen on their moorings. She signalled to him to stop. She got out and went round to his side of the car, handing him his crutches. They strolled down the narrow cobbled pier. Her hair tossed against his shoulders and she wanted to slip her right hand behind the small of his back, but thought that it might be considered too inappropriate.

Suddenly the air pulsated with loud music from several cars roaring towards the deserted yacht club, their brakes screeching brazenly as they skidded to a halt. A group of jean-clad youngsters jumped out, but Annabelle pulled Charles behind the boathouse, smiling, before making their way back to the Bentley. They drove aimlessly along the hills before pulling into the driveway of a remote country house hotel-cum-restaurant. In silence they drank tea before making their way outside, along the winding footpaths of the country hotel: thick bare woods and frosty paths engulfed them. She was laughing now, her blonde hair swinging in the mounting breeze and, as she felt his strong hand on her shoulders, she quickly pulled away, still laughing. They were silent again, and as they walked along an embankment that led away from a small pergola, she mockingly placed her tiny feet in the impressions his big shoes made in the frozen moss. Annabelle watched him carefully as he pointed to a damaged hazelnut before gazing up at the trees towering over them.

"What is it, Charles?" she asked as he handed her a damaged nut, looking at it with childlike curiosity. She felt warm beside him and she too examined the bevelled edges of the nut. She was conscious that her blonde hair was touching his cheeks. She sensed him sighing deeply and, as she watched him close his eyes, she warmed to the expression on his face. She swung her head upwards again and her heart beat faster, as she heard him say.

"It couldn't have been caused by a squirrel. They just rip open the shell with their strong teeth." But Annabelle was fighting with herself now, only half listening to his gentle drawl. Her features softened further as they sat down on a rough wooden bench that had long ago lost its green paint. She was listening to the wonder in his voice, clear and kind, while he idly pointed to the remains of abandoned patches of bound rushes, which formed platforms for water voles at the edge of the pond. She felt his hand fall on hers as they bent forward, staring at their reflection in the water. They became doubly silent. Then she felt his burning cheek against hers and his firm grip remaining on her hand for an instant before he let go again.

They sauntered back to the country house hotel in the dusk slowly, aimlessly … enjoying each other's company. Approaching the shadows of the granite archway at the door of the hotel she sensed him turn his head as she tossed her hair into his face, but then she turned away. They walked round and round the archway, aimless, secretly happy, nervous, cautious, holding on to each moment, forgetting time. The lights from the porch glistened on the dew of the short grass. She pulled her jacket tightly around her slim waist. Then, removing her Hermès scarf from around her neck, she threw it over her hair – grinning at him with chattering teeth as he read the dinner menu through the glass panel beside the entrance to the doorway. "Oh, we must try the duck," she urged as they walked inside and sat down at one of the simple square tables covered with a red gingham table cloth.

There were only two others in the dining room. The head waiter, appreciating their enjoyment, offered more duck and wine and huge portions of hot apple pie and lots of cream. Finally, after more amusing talk, they quietly said their thanksgiving prayers. They stood up and brushed their shoulders against each other, laughed – and were in the car again, heading to Coolin Castle. The cold wind howled as they wound their way up the long avenue. The huge double oak door creaked as they entered the hall. Annabelle went straight for the Aga in the large kitchen and made some hot chocolate, which they drank in silence. They stole glances at each other, afraid lest their eyes should meet.

They were standing very close to each other now and he could sense her Givenchy III perfume, the same she had worn when he'd met her at the stag hunt outside Paris less than a week ago. It wafted all about them and she closed her eyes, letting him touch her lips, before gently pushing him away.

"Goodnight, Charles. I'll show you your room." After she had shown him his quarters upstairs she entered her own room and sat down mechanically at her French dressing table. There she opened up her diary and let her arms hang down by her sides, deciding what to write. For some time she sat, staring intently at the blank page in front of her. Then slowly she carefully pulled out the slim pencil set in the side, sat bolt upright – and wrote with a firm hand in large open lettering,

"Is this love I seem to sense?" She closed her eyes then added, breaking her pencil, "Nonsense." She locked the clasp on the side, undressed, slipped into a long warm nightdress that Molly had left out for her on the radiator … and tried to sleep. Tossing and turning, she rose from her bed and peered out of the tall, dark window. Looking outside, she saw again the semi-tame red fallow deer – no longer the tiny creature that she had rescued many months ago in late spring as it'd been wandering about lost in the shrubberies on the lawn, looking for its mother. It had grown to a slightly awkward size – "Like me," she thought, with a smile on her face. In the distance branches of ghostly oaks and firs faded in the mist. The gravel glistened with a thin layer of frost, as did the odd formal gardens with their naked patches of earth. Feeling the cold creeping up along her bones she climbed back into bed and fell asleep.

* * *

Next morning all was silent as Charles walked down into the breakfast room adjoining the kitchen. Sir Jeremy – who was already down – was writing an article on his MacBook, and greeted him warmly. "Good morning, Charles. Do sit down. Don't mind me: I'm just finishing off a review for *The Telegraph*."

"Had it all been a dream? What was keeping Annabelle?" Charles thought as the houseboy brought in the toast, followed by Annabelle. "Good morning, Daddy. Good morning, Charles." She kissed her father. "I'm so pleased you've taken to the MacBook Air. You simply close the lid and everything is ready to continue when you open up the lid again, exactly as when you finished." She kissed his cheek again – and offered him her hand and pulled him out of the deep armchair, walking beside him to the breakfast table. Her wine-coloured ribbed pullover hugged her slim frame, which was set off by a faded pair of bottle green cords. Burgundy red slippers half covered her bare feet. She sat directly opposite Charles, who was straightening his napkin –but she looked only at her father at the head of the table, grinning at him.

"Charles, would you like to see the farm?" she asked eventually, still not looking at him, as she buttered her toast. "Will you have time?" she asked, still avoiding his eyes. For a moment he thought she was going to smile, but she turned towards her father again and continued talking to him. Then she suddenly turned to look at Charles directly to explain that her mother would be back much later, and suggested that they go outside and exercise some of the horses.

Charles hesitated, wondering that she might not be aware of his need for his special saddle. "That was a special handmade saddle you saw me on at Uncle Jacques's outside Paris, Annabelle. I'm not sure I'll inconvenience you by suggesting it, but a standard saddle is of little use to me after the shooting 12 years ago."

"Oh. Never mind, Charles. I thought you were so brave at Uncle Jacques's. The least I can do is to lend you my pony and trap. It's great fun, and so easy. I'm sure you'll find it fun to drive."

Once she'd seen Charles safely into her smart black and white trap – which was pulled by her pony, Haig, she mounted herself on her favourite tall mare, Whisky. She smiled sweetly at Charles for the first time that day, and sang, "Don't be vague, always call for Haig." She smiled warmly at him again. "Haig was always my favourite pony growing up," she said "And now he's so old he can only pull your wee trap. Aren't you lucky, Charles?"

Charles flicked up his eyebrows and laughed. "Our first pony was also called Haig – but he was a little devil, as he used to always attempt to ride under low branches, so he too was consigned to a trap. Yes, he too was fun then." They enjoyed sharing their reminiscences as they passed the farm yard, Charles remarking the similarity to Uncle Jacques's farmyard as they watched two workmen churning up mangolds in a large old grinder.

She bade "Good morning" to them. They returned the greeting, awkwardly touching their shapeless caps and glancing keenly from under their bowed heads at Annabelle's companion sitting in the pony trap. As they left the cobblestoned farmyard Annabelle simply grinned at them without a further word.

The short manicured grass along the back avenue gave way to the longer natural grass stumps as they approached the river. She did not speak, and the frightened appearance of a blue hare seemed to intensify the cold hollow feeling which began to possess them both. They continued on for a mile in total silence and then rode back along the side avenue back to the farmyard, where Annabelle handed over her mare and Charles his pony and trap.

* * *

Once back upstairs in his room there was little for him to do: everything was already packed. Leaving an envelope on the dresser and signing the guest book, he said goodbye to the family and drove off. He cast a final glance in the rear mirror of the car. Annabelle was standing alone on the gravel. She was not waving but just as he began to lose sight of her he thought he saw her hand shoot up.

Chapter Twenty-Nine

A nnabelle lowered her hand as Charles's Bentley went out of sight, and she stamped her feet as she began to cry. She promptly rushed upstairs to her room, starting to write him a letter:

Dear Charles,

I have a problem. Not a problem, as such. I suppose … that is … it's just … what I am trying to say is … that there will be no afterwards for us. I have a horror of getting involved with anybody … no particular reason … nothing.

I realise that it was inexcusable of me to encourage you. Having you here, accepting your lovely presents, giving you false impressions … but I enjoyed it … not the deceiving, because I wasn't then … but you, actually.

I should have told you before you went, told you before I left France, told you what I felt when you had only just arrived … Oh, Charles, this all sounds so frightfully prosaic … I want to give you a great big hug and a kiss, and laughingly whisper, *"Vas t'en, mon choux. Adieux."*

There is a reason, actually – but it is so complicated I should never get round to expressing it … it is just that I undergo a type of mental struggle … a torment … torture … a *"Je ne sais pas quoi"* - and the only solution appears to be to eradicate the cause.

"Eh voila. Tu comprends?" I wish so much that you should.

Love, Annabelle.

* * *

Charles – who had motored all the way back to his club in Edinburgh to be ready for the discussions on Monday morning concerning his family affairs with his Scottish investment manager – finally arrived one day later at his family's Scottish shooting estate, which lay south of the Highlands near Perth. A pile of damp letters awaited him on the flagstones in the hall. He instantly guessed the author of one recent letter, written in a clear open hand, and his heart started racing wildly as he tore it open.

As he read and reread Annabelle's letter his face paled. He searched for an explanation, examining each word. His head reeled as he caught sight of a face in the large mirror, which was mounted over a colourful Bellini-signed scaglioni-topped table and depicted an Italian summer festival scene. The face was a sick, pale, hollow face: it was his face. He swung himself towards the main staircase, went upstairs, supported by creaking mahogany banisters and searched for writing paper in his old room.

Everything was damp, cold and unlived-in. He read the letter again, walked carefully downstairs and then shouted out loud, filling the hall with painful fury. "Oh, Annabelle. What are we up to?" He spoke to the walls, the ceilings … and his wailing voice sent whisperings through the ghostly mansion. He snatched at the telephone in the hall and asked the exchange to get him the Beauchamp number.

"Hello … Annabelle?"

"No, this is her mother, Lady Beauchamp. Who is speaking?"

"Oh … hello. This is Charles Russell-Lafitte, Lady Beauchamp."

"Hello, Charles. How are you? I am so sorry I missed seeing you again after the weekend. I'm afraid Annabelle has gone back to Oxford with her father. Can I give her a message?"

"Yes ... I mean ... No. No, thank you .... it's ... it's all right ... Thank you again for a lovely stay. I was sorry to have missed you ... Goodbye." He put down the telephone lamely, dazed and surprised, and then became angry with himself. He snatched at one of his old yellow-coloured raincoats and a dark hat that were still hanging in the hall, and swung himself outside.

* * *

That evening, back at his club, Charles (having changed his damp clothes) telephoned Oxford and finally succeeded in getting Annabelle from the porter's lodge in Wolfson College. She was cool, self-possessed, and he – the moment he heard her voice – floundered, not knowing what to think. This set the tone for a series of monotones, hesitations and prolonged suffocating pauses.

"Well, Charles", Annabelle finally said. "I don't think we have anything further to say, do we?" Astonished and confused, he replied with a meaningless, "No ... Yes ... Yes." There was a further pause as he said an awkward "Goodbye."

But then suddenly she added, "Charles, don't telephone me here any more, please. It's so awkward for the porter to get me to the telephone. You do understand? If you like, do write." There was a long pause. "Charles?" She sounded puzzled, with a higher pitch to her hazy voice. "Yes?" he answered weakly, and then sighed heavily. "Oh, Annabelle."

Beyond himself, he replaced the receiver. Frustration and anger welled up inside him, and yet within 10 minutes he felt able to sit down to dinner at the members' table in his club. He joined and listened in to the conversations which had just taken place at the relatively new Scottish parliament while his mind started to formulate a letter to a girl whom he hardly knew and yet who, somehow, had managed to captivate him.

After coffee at the members' table he bid his fellow diners good night. Then went upstairs to his room where he sat down at a writing table, staring out of the window into the womblike night. Finally he wrote:

My dear Annabelle,

Your beauty, your fine spirit and truly wonderful candid nature have taken me out of myself and transplanted me melting, blinding, into your sweet person. I felt, in your presence, so...?

He stopped, thought for a long time, was going to put down the word, infatuated, but instead left the space blank. Then he tore up the letter and started again.

Dearest Annabelle,

The multitude of embracing sentiments I feel within me become commonplace as I try to set them down on paper. But for me to feel as I do, an eternal bachelor, there must – oh Annabelle – there surely must be some reciprocating spark. Perhaps unwanted, ignored?

Oh, Annabelle, it is useless trying to put down on paper sentiments which in the labyrinth of one's mind have a quality and a lightness – a beauty so genuine – that they go beyond mere expression.

He sighed, the sentences getting longer, more complex and losing all natural reason. The grandfather clock chimed midnight outside his bedroom door and each stroke brought him back to reality. He looked at the chaos of the hastily-scribbled pages at his feet and he tore them all up before falling on his bed, exhausted. The next several days were spent between the club, his shooting lodge, the distilleries and the investment houses. He wrote letters and more letters, as if he had become a split personality. Yet he longed for more letters, but forced himself nonetheless to concentrate coldly on his investment affairs. He devoured each letter from Annabelle as if it were the best possible tonic:

> Charles darling,
>
> What a pleasant surprise to find your letter awaiting me when I got back from my cousin's last night. Was more surprised when I read its contents. Oh, Charles, what long cumbersome sentences: you must explain them to me some time … much too complicated for me to decipher in spite of my reading them over and over.
>
> Love, Annabelle.

And so they corresponded, until Charles realised how besotted he'd become. He admonished himself: he'd never given proper thought to Annabelle's daily pressures of long, demanding essays and her tutorials at her Oxford graduate college. Then the wood suddenly stood out from the trees and he saw that it was in the very accumulation of both their letters that the real expression of truth was to be found. He saw it all quite clearly now and yet he feared that the next moment his own vibrant feelings might dismiss all objectivity again. With that, he sent her a final letter to Coolin Castle:

> Dearest Annabelle,
>
> I shall miss you, miss writing to you, miss spending every free waking moment thinking about you … but I see now that's just how it is. You still are and will ever remain my dearest caterpillar.
>
> Let us make a simple pact: to pray for each other every day and for an end to the destruction of our families. I am now leaving your beautiful country for America, for a weekend with Cousin George.
>
> Love, Charles.

At Coolin Castle the postman, as was his custom, entered by a small side door that gave on to the kitchen and the warm Aga. After following Sir Jeremy into the kitchen for a cup of tea he held the mail and the morning newspapers firmly in his gloved hand. He began by taking off his gloves, rubbing his purple hands furiously together.

"Fair terrible, the storm last night, sir," he commented, before taking the proffered cup of tea – which he downed in seconds. Completely satisfied, he returned to the freezing weather outside on his bicycle, hailing his farewells. "Top of the morning, to you, sir." His loud Scottish twang was full of joy.

Sir Jeremy glanced at the handwriting on the envelopes before opening *The Telegraph* and squatting snugly in his favourite armchair near the Aga.

"Good morning, Daddy," Annabelle said as she bounded into the breakfast room, pecking her father's cheek. She had taken the train from Oxford the previous evening for the long weekend.

"Some mail for you again this morning, my dear – and there, on the sideboard, lots more … Quite a correspondence you're having," her father chided playfully, as he settled himself down to *The Telegraph* again.

Annabelle collected all her letters from the sideboard and sat down. "Isn't Charles a dear?" she sang with pride, "So extraordinarily persistent." She continued eagerly to tear open the letters but then she became silent as she read and reread the contents of his last letter. Her poached egg congealed as she read his last letter again, and without a word she slipped quietly up to her room. She looked out the window of her bedroom for a long time, and suddenly burst out crying without any semblance of control. "Oh, Charles," she sighed, her tearful head on her hands. She sat up at her writing table, vaguely reaching for some paper. Then she started to write, but stopped. She tore up the letter, started the whole procedure again … and then repeated it and tore it up again.

Finally she wrote him the following letter:

Dearest Charles,

You hypersensitive idiot. You know perfectly well - or you ought to know how I feel towards you. Dearest Charles, how tremendously sad you would appear and — after such a dramatic letter — how helpless you make me feel. What am I to say, Charles dear? What can I say other than it is I who should feel hurt? … Oh, and I do. I do. Funny, isn't it? That I should feel like this in spite of … Oh, Charles dearest, what a mutt I've been. And you? You weigh so heavily on my thoughts - but now I am really frightfully serious. For once you're thinking … It's just that I never expected to get involved so … with you …

Oh, Charles, you must know how I feel towards you … Oh, and Charles, dear you were so darlingly persistent. It flatters us no end … Wicked, aren't we?

Darling, I too — like you — have become quite fascinated, actually. But how can you be so obvious? Really rather unusual, you know? Oh, but do write, do phone, do call … I so long to see you and I do so hope you haven't changed dreadfully.

Love, Annabelle.

But her letter arrived at a large forlorn uninhabited empty shooting lodge in the Highlands.

Chapter Thirty

The flight from Edinburgh back to Paris took less than an hour, after which Charles left the new jet in its designated bay at Orly airport and went in search of Fred his pilot in the adjoining building. There, as previously arranged, he would also meet Marie St Julien and Mark de Beaumont in the departure lounge.

* * *

That preceding damp Saturday Jean Etchips had become drowsy from the metronomic clicks on the windscreen made by his wipers as he waited outside Charles's sister Anne's house on the Avenue Foch. He'd persisted, awaiting a reply to his email from Dr Humburger and hoping to avoid a parking ticket. He sat up abruptly when the noise of the sharp electronic squeak on his mobile combined with the roar of a powerful car hurtling past him through Anne's gates. "That was Charles Russell-Lafitte in his inimitable Bentley," he'd whispered out loud (he was astonished) as he tried to understand the vital instructions from Dr Humburger, which came through by email and which were subsequently confirmed by voice on his telephone. Etchips listened in stunned silence, as he'd seemed to have agreed to be complicit in the actual execution of a multiple murder without actually having said so.

Then he felt his blood draining from his face as he finally committed himself to say, "Yes, of course, *Herr Doctor.*" With that he clicked shut his mobile and drove hurriedly to Orly airport. By the time he'd arrived at the airport and had scanned the private parking bays of the aircraft there, he looked up to just catch the Lafitte jet departing. He finally managed to find the French version of the Lafitte Bentley. He had earlier ascertained from Dr Humburger that Charles would be flying out from Orly next Saturday with Marie St Julien and Marc de Beaumont to Kentucky.

Etchips had become painfully aware that blackmail was indeed a powerful weapon now that he was himself on the receiving end. As instructed, he was to collect a large Jiffy bag at the poste restante office at the airport's PTT, together with another, smaller bag – from which, as instructed – he should remove a pilot's hat. He should put on that hat and walk to the designated bay after the returning de Lafitte jet had been refuelled and was made ready for its scheduled take-off for the USA.

It was absolutely vital that he should be there on time next Saturday, since Charles would be flying back some time that day from Scotland prior to flying out again to Kentucky, with possibly other cousins. The more the merrier. It was essential that the bomb be planted accurately, as per the instructions on the email.

* * *

"It can travel faster than the speed of sound," Mark said, holding out his hand for Marie, as they boarded the Lafitte jet which had landed at Orly from Edinburgh airport and had already been refuelled that Saturday afternoon. Charles turned to the pilot.

"It'll be pretty dark over the east coast tonight, Fred. The main computer software is not scheduled to be repaired before Sunday night." After opening the cabin door, Charles again turned to Fred. "See you later," he said, and joined the others in the more relaxed atmosphere behind the cockpit.

"Absolute chaos as far as Kentucky, for a whole week," said Charles. "No power and no communications until Sunday night. George will be in his element."

"But how will he cope?" asked Marie, "Without electricity?"

"He's fully equipped on his standby and he's been wanting to try out this for years. He will finally be able to test his standby electrical systems."

Charles continued speaking fondly of his cousin. "His popularity will be really tested this week. His hunt ball, although weird and wonderful, is patronised by most of the hunting fraternity in the adjoining states. They'll fly over their own horses from as far as Maryland. They'll all be there tonight."

"How many guests are expected tonight?" asked Mark. "Anyone's guess, really, but the usual form is between 150 to 200." They continued talking, and Charles abandoned his original idea of taking the controls of the jet himself.

Mark, as heir to one of the founding families of the Banque de Lafitte, had spent some time working in private French and American banks. "I'm also now hoping to spend a few years working alongside my semi-retired father," he told Charles. "Good. My uncle's almost persuaded me to do the same," said Charles, and for the next few hours they discussed the future strategy of the families. By evening, Charles looked inside the control cabin to bid Fred an early night. Marie had retired earlier, and Mark now retired to his own compartment.

The steady hum of the faster-than-the-speed-of-sound aircraft reassured Charles as he retired to the compartment at the back of the aircraft just above the undercarriage. He retrieved a sleeping bag from one of the cupboards and placed it on the floor in front of his small desk. As soon as Charles put his head down he sensed an almost inaudible ticking sound. It didn't alarm him, since it acted as a perfect metronome for reading his mother's poem, which his father had given him. His mother's love poem moved him and he folded it up again, lay back and fell asleep for a few hours.

* * *

A few hours later the voice of Fred sounded loudly throughout the aircraft. "We will be landing in Kentucky in one hour's time." Charles woke up with a start, fully alert. Again the faint ticking sound from below registered with him. Had he dismissed it earlier too readily? He immediately started shaving with his electric Braun – then scooped up the sleeping bag, looked for his crutches and stood up, looking puzzled. After dressing he bent down again, and removed the floor covering. The ticking sound continued more distinctly now, and after a quick consultation with Fred in the cockpit, they found the operations manual.

"I know it sounds ridiculous, Fred", Charles said, "But put the jet on automatic pilot and come back with me and listen for yourself." A detailed search ensued at the back with the aid of the aircraft manual. Fred lifted the carpet again and removed an aluminium floor panel. Then he got down on to his hands and knees and listened. "Yes," Fred said, looking up. "Very strange - doesn't seem normal."

They became very quiet. Fred checked the manual again and said, "Charles, why don't we carry out a mirror search of the undercarriage? We can do it from the cockpit." Charles soon manipulated the special series of hydraulic flaps fitted with illuminated mirrors and searchlights that allowed a complete scan of the aircraft's undercarriage in mid flight. He continued searching inch by inch then said excitedly,

"There. Underneath the right undercarriage on the bottom left-hand corner. A slender aluminium cube - clearly visible, with the yellow timer button I read about in *What's New?* a few weeks ago. It's planned to go off as we go in to land."

"Five minutes to landing." Fred's professional voice rang out reassuringly through the aircraft. Charles spoke with a determined calm beside him. "Dump the fuel." Fred waited for an explanation, but Charles started to unbuckle his seat belt and addressed his pilot again. "This is a totally unorthodox plan, Fred, but frankly I'm not going to let you carry the can for this one." Fred was already out of his seat, thinking this was no time for a confrontation and gave way instantly, aware that Charles regularly passed the highest proficiency tests available.

"Thanks, Fred. That explosive device is scheduled to go off as soon as the undercarriage comes down for landing." Charles seemed calm. "We're going to skim over the cluster of young trees which border George's landing strip," he said. "If we come in fast, we'll rip off the bomb, hopefully, before it can do any major damage."

But as the other cousins had opened the cockpit door they turned white. It was the first time they had heard the word bomb. Charles turned to look at Marie and Mark. "We're taking a calculated risk here. I suggest you both go and sit directly behind the cockpit and take up the emergency position. This could be fatal, so say one for me too." They then kissed each other in turn. Marie blessed herself and Mark squeezed her hand before taking up the crash position. Mark blessed himself and made no further comment.

"God bless you, Charles," Marie whispered before closing the door. Then she turned to Mark, smiling sweetly. "And you too, darling." She closed her eyes serenely and started to pray.

As Charles took over the controls he felt the enormity of his responsibility. "Fasten seat belts. We're dumping fuel now," he announced. During the next five minutes there was an agonised silence, wherein real time seemed to disappear. As he dived down below the cloud belt only a chink of moonlight was visible. Charles could not see any landing lights in the distance and thought, "Where are those young saplings? Surely George would've told me if they'd been cut down."

He only had enough fuel to climb once more. Rely on instinct, but no - that was too risky. George used to come in from the south west … but I'm not sure … it was so long ago." The jet flew over the end of what Charles thought was the runway, but there was still no sight of any young trees as the aircraft roared back into the clouds. Suddenly Charles remembered. Yes, the saplings were planted in the south west. "We're going in now. Continue your prayers."

The soft drone of the descent was interrupted by the sharp acceleration as the jet raced through the dark clouds.

Below all was darkness with no trace of the runway lights. Charles's face blanched. "Reserve lights," he called out in desperation, as the plane continued to dive. "Where are those trees? They must be there," Charles called out. Every impulse was urging him to pull out of his dive, but still he descended. Then, for a split second, he caught the reflection of ice crystals on top of what must be the young trees he'd been looking for. He slammed home the lever to level off, and dramatically increased speed again. The newly-bonded elasticised alloys seemed to hold as the jet screamed, slicing off the ice and snow from the top of the young pines. The violence of the buffeting and a loud bang of the dislodged bomb rocked the jet out of control.

Charles fought with the flaps of the undercarriages and reduced speed sharply. This made the buffeting even worse. "Report damage. We're going back up until we assess the situation," Charles ordered, perspiring with concentration as the aircraft lurched upwards with a violent roar. Fred feverishly tried to operate some of the damaged mirrored flaps.

"Right undercarriage only partially down. Torn tail wing. Scorch marks," Fred reported professionally. "Good. We're going back down and landing," said Charles in a cool voice. Fred had now managed to get to grips with the emergency searchlights on the jet and they could both now just make out the outline of the runway, which was dimly spreading a faint sheen of light just below the ice and snow. The noise of the vibration screeching throughout the aircraft was dramatically increased by the shuddering of the plane.

Charles could feel the jet going out of control again. He felt that the craft might shatter itself into tiny pieces. He forced the aircraft on to its left undercarriage, which seemed intact and operable. He felt a momentary bouncing sensation, and tried to level off the jet as it lurched violently in the opposite direction on to the extremity of the right wing with its empty fuel tank. The aircraft spun around like a top, scraping the ground. Thousands of sparks illuminated the wreckage. Localised flames started to spread from the torn wing. "Everybody out," Charles roared as the spinning jet shuddered to a halt.

The heavy fumes of aviation fuel burst into the main cabin as Fred swung open the stepped door. As the others ran down the steps Charles hesitated. He hit the red button over the door and a cascade of water mist jetted down, partially clearing the air. He reached back into the cockpit with his crutches, grabbed his overnight bag and – using the overhead winch – lowered himself down on the tarmac. Without hesitation he flung himself to join the others scrambling on the snow-covered grass bordering the runway.

Charles looked back once more and saw a plume of flames creeping up to the other fuel tank. "Dive down," he roared. A fraction of a second later a great ball of fire consumed the jet. "Face the ground," Charles roared again, as huge balls of black smoke rose high above them. Through the freezing night air they could soon hear the makeshift siren on the converted Jeep hurtling towards them.

Coughing furiously, Fred helped Charles and his cousins into the old Jeep and then jumped in beside the driver before the open Jeep raced back to the makeshift watchtower.

"Well, that was thrilling," Charles said flippantly, trying to make light of the situation. Nobody replied. Their thoughts were dark, as they all knew that they had just escaped certain death by a whisker. Charles remained silent too, sensing that it was part of something bigger. But why would anyone pick on Mark or Marie or Fred? Or was it just him who was still the intended victim? Who had planted that bomb, and why?

Charles recalled his earlier conversation with Uncle Jacques in the boot room of the chateau. Jacques had been on the point of recognising the Swiss voice on that tape. What was the name of that man?

Chapter Thirty-One

C harles stood up, supported by his crutches in the freezing Jeep as it approached the colonnaded house of Gordonston Manor, and waved calmly. All in the house looked out in disbelief as the Jeep hurtled towards them from the fireball. George Gordonston-Lafitte was already running down the steps: his six-foot-six frame towered over everyone.

"Everyone all right, C B? You OK, Marie? Hello, Mark."

Charles embraced his best friend and cousin (who had always called him Charles Boy when they had been boys and had reduced that to the simple initials C B), and whispered, "That, George, was not an accident. It was a bomb planted in Paris. But until we get the facts it remains an ordinary accident. So don't stop the party, whatever you do."

"Point taken, but everyone is so concerned, C B. Hang on. I'll make an announcement from the Jeep." Standing up beside Charles in the Jeep, he put his arms up in the air and waved them slowly up and down until he got everyone's attention. He raised his voice.

"As you can see, Cousin Charles and everyone else is safe". The guests began to clap, but he raised his arms again. "I have received instructions to not – I repeat not – stop the party." With that there were great shouts of joy. The windows were closed and the music resumed. "But who would do such a thing, C B? What could be their motive?" asked George, still bewildered.

"It's a European problem. We'll deal with it over there when we get back after the weekend," Charles said, adding,

"Sorry to make such a dramatic entrance, George. Not my usual style," he chuckled. Then, seeing Marie was cold and quaking with shock, he tugged at George's dinner jacket and nodded towards her. George immediately saw the dilemma and removed his black jacket, putting it over Marie's shoulders.

"Anything you want done? Don't let me do it, C .B. I'm rather jittery myself," said George, relieved that everyone had escaped. Charles looked at his cousin fondly, laughing with relief. "I'm sure our pilot Fred can handle the aviation inspectors with your chaps at the control tower. All of whom, by the way, were splendid. I might as well own up and say I took over from Fred as acting pilot towards the end," Charles finished quietly, as they'd reached the top of the steps.

With that George swung around. "Aha. But that explains everything, C B. Yes, I can hear you now on Monday, knocking on Uncle Jacques's door, "Come in."

"Ahem - Uncle Jacques, I thought you ought to know. That the new $30 million jet, you know – the silver one, just released from our Canadian factory – well it's gone," and your uncle replying, "Gone? Charles, my boy, you are a bit older now. You seem to have grown up to be even taller than me. Do please sit down, my boy, so that I can strangle you properly."

George, with his hands around Charles's neck, looked fiercely at Marie and Mark and in a gargling version of Charles's voice, continued the comedy. "Uncle Jacques, please don't. You're killing me and I haven't yet signed my preliminary report for the insurance company." By the time they had reached the outer entrance of the main door and stopped laughing, Charles and the others' faces were less drawn. "What about the press, George?"

"Most of the Sunday morning papers won't be appearing. The blackout this weekend is really bringing out the best in everybody, CB." Then he stopped, walking outside again. "Look. Isn't our home-brew electricity fine?" George swung his arms up towards the lights of the main entrance, to the hall and up to the glittering chandeliers of the huge stairs to the first landing. All the lights of the 18th-century house blazed as normal.

"It took just less than half an hour to get our mini station going. I proved them all wrong, C B - Dad was pleased too, because everything in his greenhouse would have gone for a Burton." George had drawn himself up proudly, and added, "But I think I'll ask for all the gates around the estate to be locked. It's the TV crews who'll worry me once they're back on the air - reportedly by tomorrow night."

As they reached the banisters of the main hall staircase, George seemed relieved that the party was back in full swing.

"Here, you guys," he turned to Mark and Marie, "I expect you'd like to get changed. Then let's have fun." There was a deadly silence. George began to backtrack, looking at C B for support. He started again, "Err, maybe not. Why don't you retire, so you'll be all ready for the hunt in the morning? Follow me," he said, as he led the way upstairs. Then he whispered, "But C B, you're not getting off that lightly. You're seeing this one through with me."

Charles laughed, "I've so much adrenalin rushing around after that near miss, I couldn't possible sleep now."

"Great," said George with gusto. "We'll say hello to my parents first. They're anxious about you. There they are," he said, as they walked downstairs. After a few pleasantries, minimising the crash, George led his guests upstairs again to show them their rooms.

"Stokes here will find anything you want, Mark. He's not good with your sort of stuff, Marie, I'm afraid, but I'll have to ask my half-sister Georgiana to come up and help." Marie smiled as she watched an apologetic George with his bulky frame trying to close the drawer of a tiny boudoir table in her room. "Thank you so much, George. It is so kind of you, but I'll manage." Then she firmly closed the door behind them. As a European she was unaccustomed to this happy-go-lucky American generosity, but already loved George's generous ways.

"Don't know how you survived that inferno, C B." George slapped his cousin on the back as they sauntered down to the landing. He said this with a slight American accent, which blended perfectly with his former Etonian drawl. "It's good to have you back in one piece. I like your aluminium crutches." They continued downstairs where Georgiana, George's stepsister, and his distant cousin Caroline Conolly-Lafitte met them coming out of the ballroom. "Georgiana." Charles embraced her. She had been exclusively educated in America and had a big open smile that invited instant trust. She had narrow shoulders on an otherwise slim body, which made her an ideal model for the angular Chanel clothes that she occasionally modelled at charity functions.

Tonight she wore a simple black velvet dress with a single strand of real pearls. She immediately turned to her companion, who was wearing a similar outfit. "Caroline, of course you know Charles. She is your very distant cousin, who shares our Lafitte name." She smiled as she instantly sensed the electricity as Charles embraced Caroline fondly.

"Oh, Charles." Caroline returned Charles's embrace with warmth. "I'm so glad none of you were hurt." Her intelligent brown eyes, set wide apart, smiled into his ... before Charles embraced Caroline in turn a second time.

"You're both looking so well, Caroline and Georgiana. Where're we hunting tomorrow?" Charles asked excitedly.

Georgiana's face lit up, and she started to go into the greatest detail of the country where the hounds would draw, including the Mississippi run. As she looked at Charles's expression a frown appeared on her face, and she stole a quick glance at her cousin Caroline. "Someone else asked me that exact same question, only a week ago," she said, trying to remember. "Now, who was it? ... Yes, at the saddler's."

"What's wrong, Georgiana?" asked Charles. "Yes, that's where it was - at the local saddler. A total stranger." She looked at Caroline. "Come to think of it, he looked so like you, Charles. It's uncanny. He was dressed entirely differently, of course, but really ... he could have been an identical twin. So handsome." She was looking intently at Caroline and Charles now. "No, Georgiana - my twin, as you know, died at birth," Charles countered.

"But seriously, Charles, he asked me exactly the same questions. He said he was from New York, spending a holiday here in Kentucky, doing research on something or other. He seemed such a nice fellow. We ... I was with Caroline at the time and we very nearly asked him to come to the ball tonight, actually."

Georgiana laughed, with the faintest blush of joy appearing from nowhere on her fair cheeks. "He was even more tanned than you, and I thought he had a touch of an Italian accent. So charming, these Italians, aren't they?"

"*Fantastico*," said Charles, swinging down his right hand courteously.

Georgiana went pale as he bowed, as if she'd seen a ghost. But what with George hopping on his feet and flinging his hands about, wanting to interrupt them, she didn't say anything.

"Georgiana, Caroline ... the jet's a complete write-off and your cousin Marie St Julien hasn't got a thing to wear. Could you possibly rustle something up?" George said, and the saddle shop incident was forgotten for the time being.

"Of course. How silly of us," both girls said in unison. They turned and began to run upstairs. "Charles, we must talk later," they both called up, leaning over the banisters, looking at Charles fixedly. Charles turned to George. "Aren't they wonderful girls? Come on. I've something special for you."

"Goody goody gumdrops. Take the waiting out of wanting," George mocked, rubbing his hands together like a child. "It's in my holdall, which I managed to save at the last moment. That new jet from our Canadian plant is - was - an absolute dream. It saved our lives, you know. I say, George," Charles nodded down to the large door of the drawing room off the hallway. "I didn't know Annabelle had been invited."

"Where? I beg your pardon Colonel, Where, C B?"

"Over there, with the blonde hair, sitting beside - is it? Yes, Old Hetherington," said Charles.

"Oh, that Annabelle. Oh, yes. She's a stunner and a neighbour. Often stays next door with Caroline when she's over. Too much of a bluestocking for me, C B. I was talking to her earlier. She intends doing an Oxford postgrad in English literature, you know." George looked sideways at his cousin and grinned. "Way out of my league, I'm afraid. More your type, though?" It was the second time Charles had seen Annabelle out of her hunting kit without her top hat. A stream of long blonde hair enveloped her shoulders, sloping down to the top of her low cut, wine-coloured ball gown. Spellbound by her beauty, he continued to look at her until a throng of guests moved out of the drawing room, interrupting his view. "I was actually only introduced to her at Uncle Jacques's lawn meet and subsequently last week. I'd no idea she was coming here," Charles said.

George raised his eyebrows. "Pleasant surprise? Dreadful surprise? Or just a surprise? Don't answer that. By the way, how is that workhorse of ours, Uncle Jacques? Does he ever stop?"

"Oh, he was about to finish off his stag on Saturday, when acting as huntsman for the day, just before I left early for Anne's drinks at the Avenue Foch." They both went up the back stairs to the left wing of the house, to the room that which had been designated Charles's since his boyhood. George ambled upstairs, matching Charles's laborious climbing speed perfectly.

Nothing had changed and was just as Charles last remembered it. "I got Stokes to bring your hand luggage over from the Jeep," George said on entering the room. "Stokes, don't bother unpacking," urged Charles, smiling warmly at the old manservant. "I expect you've more than enough to do tonight. How are you?"

The old man looked at him for a moment, not recognising Charles with his crutches. Then his eyes lit up, a grin spreading across his face. "It's you, Master Charles. How are you, sir? My old eyes are none too good." Charles nodded as he took and unzipped his overnight bag, with the words, "George, It's here somewhere." He screwed up his face and dug deeper. "Got it," he finally said, and handed the carefully-wrapped Hermès package to George, which the tall young man immediately ripped apart.

"What? Stokes, look at this beautiful riding crop. Thanks a million, C B. I'll use it first thing tomorrow morning. By the way, don't bother stirring before 10.30 for the hunt. Mass, by the way, is at nine in Mummy's chapel. Oh no - actually that's wrong. It's 9.30 on a Sunday. Do you want to go? Shall I get

Stokes to wake you?" George looked fixedly at his manservant. Charles nodded agreement before they continued slowly downstairs again. George spoke up as he pushed aside a long mahogany table which sealed off the top landing from the main staircase.

"I say, C B. Look, Sir Henry Steere's just arrived. He's our new joint master of foxhounds, d'y'know?" George nodded towards the hall door, where an old man and a young girl were shaking hands with George's parents. "Come on," George cried out, nudging Charles, "Our new joint master will have a few words to say to you, C B."

"Really? Do tell. is that his daughter?"

"That's his new wife, you twit. Come on, let me introduce you." When they arrived downstairs George made the introductions.

"Lady Fiona, Sir Henry Steere … I should like you to meet my cousin and best friend, Charles Russell-Lafitte … CB for short." Sir Henry's face paled as if he'd seen a ghostly apparition. "Ah, how do you do?" he said, instantly switching his eyes back to George, calling on all the resources of his MI6 training by inventing a story on the spot.

"Capital run you missed on Wednesday, George. It must have been a one-mile point before the hounds crashed into their fox. Splendid run, I'm told." Sir Henry continued to kick for touch, not daring to look at Charles, thinking, "How could he have escaped from both the sniper's bullet in Paris and the smouldering wreckage lying outside? Desperately eager to fall in with any ruse which would give him time to collect himself, he continued to prattle on. "And then they found him again in Astor's wood, though they soon lost him. But it wasn't long before the hounds hit his line again, and once they got him out into the open he didn't last long."

Lady Fiona, who was attractive in a horsy sort of way, had spent her entire childhood at pony clubs in England. She looked at her husband and pouted. "Harry, have I missed something frightfully good? You are making all this up." But to her husband's enormous relief, and before anyone could say a further word, their little group was pulled apart as the band played a Paul Jones. Dancers in a long chain of winding bodies propelled them from the hall towards the ballroom. Charles immediately withdrew himself from the swirling circle of bodies as they entered ballroom. Suddenly the music stopped and there, in front of him, stood Annabelle. She carried her head high and her pale, powder blue eyes were laughing. She wore only the slightest trace of make-up. Golden, corn-like hair streaked back from her high brow.

The music had changed to a foxtrot and Charles swung forward on his crutches. "Would you like to dance?" he said – and his voice sounded curiously strange to him, as if he was hearing it for the first time … like a schoolboy on his first date. The sparkle in her eyes gave way to concern as she thought of his crutches and the wreckage outside, and she said, in a deadpan voice, "You've been busy."

"It was only a test, which didn't altogether fail, "he replied, handing her his right crutch with a grin. "Put it under your left armpit as an extra support," which she did with a smile and without protest, saying, "I dare say you were the pilot?"

"Right in one. The crash was exclusively my fault."

"And do you always insist on being so exclusive?" Charles felt her eyes laughing at him, daring him on.

"Wasn't that fun last week?" he ventured. "I'm not sure what you're referring to," she said. Her eyes still dared him, and he added quickly, "I meant our visit last week and Uncle Jacques's lawn meet?"

"I know," she said. "I apologise for borrowing your Arab 12 times."

Charles smiled as she continued, "Apart from last week, do you never visit Scotland any more?" She threw back her head, her sparking eyes catching the light from an overhead chandelier, and then she added accusingly, in a mock Scottish brogue, "Or are you a true absentee landlord?" A mysterious smile melted on her full lips. "Guilty in one." He added, "Why? Your place in Scotland is nice too."

"Oh, nice, is it?" she answered, with that same contradictory smile. Her eyes – which up till now had glinted with mockery – softened as she met his, and he could sense that she was inviting him to look at her as she was. He could see that she felt undaunted by the searching inquiry that he was making, as he felt the overwhelming warmth of her nature all about him. He held her closer, saying, "I don't suppose you mind supporting my extra weight? You see I'll have to lean on you more than before I was shot 12 years ago."

"Lean as much as you like, Charles. Although, having no brothers or sisters, I'm not very experienced. But I have had lots of practice in many three-legged races, which I always won, by the way."

They both laughed and she closed her eyes as they danced on. He saw that her eyes were still sparkling when she opened them. As if not wishing to lose the ecstasy of the moment he saw her close them slowly and he felt her warmth engulf him – but not for long, as he heard her amused voice demanding, "What shall we talk about now, Charles?" She continued to smile, raising her chin a little as she said, "I'm waiting for an answer, Charles."

"Annabelle," he countered, pronouncing her name emphatically, seeing her lips part into a full, challenging smile.

Without warning, the music of the slow foxtrot merged into another loud Paul Jones. As he withdrew, she quickly handed him back the crutch with outstretched hands as the dance became frantic. She flung her arms about wildly, inadvertently brushing his cheek, and she laughed at his surprise as she was pulled away. "Goodbye, Charles," she teased, looking intently at him for a moment. Then, with a sharp jerk, she tossed her blonde hair around. The ballroom thronged with reeling couples and spilled over into the adjoining library, which attracted another set with soft music from a different orchestra.

Chapter Thirty-Two

C harles sat down quietly in the library but catching sight of his distant cousin Dr Caroline, he promptly asked her to dance the next foxtrot. He was amazed how she managed to dance with him, taking one of his crutches and making him feel thoroughly at ease. She insisted that they should dance again after a short rest, after she was asked by another member of the hunt for a dance. Charles remembered his father's advice when he caught one more exquisite glimpse of Caroline in profile as she danced away, before familiar voices hailed him from the chequered hallway. As he passed underneath the architraves of the panelled doorway he saw his French cousin Marie trying to catch his attention.

"I thought you were asleep," Charles greeted Marie St Julien. "I did try, but I couldn't, so I thought I'd review my guest list for the wedding," Marie said, showing off her new dress. "Georgiana and Caroline were so helpful, lending me this fine black dress in case I changed my mind. You, Charles, must bring those beautiful cousins Annabelle and Caroline along with you. Annabelle's in love with you, you know?" Charles looked at Marie, completely taken aback. "Annabelle? But, we only met once – last week at Uncle Jacques's lawn meet, and for a subsequent short weekend in Scotland."

"Think back, Charles. You've known her since she was a baby - and you certainly met her and Caroline when we were all in our teens. Remember Uncle Charlemagne's diamond wedding anniversary in Suvretta?" She looked fondly at Dr Caroline, who had now joined them, and then at Charles. "You were put in charge of all the children under 14. Remember one little girl who insisted on crawling all over you? Well, that little girl is now our Cambridge graduate, Annabelle." He looked at Marie and Caroline for a long time, his face crumpling up with a happy innocence which he hadn't experienced since he was a boy.

"But she can't be. I do remember a highly persistent intelligent little girl. I called her … what was it? Yes, the caterpillar," he said, a faraway look in his eyes. "That's her," said Marie and Caroline jointly. "We were both there."

"Goodness. You girls," said Charles. Still lost in thought, he kissed them both again. "You're angels. Real angels."

Something had clicked in his mind as the girls laughed, but Charles changed the conversation as he addressed Marie. "I'm so pleased for you and Mark. He's one of the finest chaps I know. His father's been a real friend to our family for yonks. That, Caroline, is an Americanism I learned from George. I spent a term with him and Mark at Harvard."

Marie's eyes sparkled and she flushed with happiness, looking at both her cousins in turn. "Oh Charles, don't you think Mark's madly attractive?"

"Can't help you there, Marie," he said, and switched his eyes to Caroline, who simply smiled warmly at him.

Marie, overcome with emotion replied, "Seriously, Charles, I couldn't keep my eyes off him at Anne's party. I'd die if we were ever separated again."

As they all looked at each other they realised they were thinking about the near miss and the wreckage lying in the fields outside. Marie smiled sweetly, giving him a peck on the cheek. "Thank you, Charles, for saving us," she said, as they all turned to watch George strolling over. The music became louder as yet more doors were opened. Swarms of dancers swirled around the ballroom, overflowing into the main hall and the dining room. Charles faced his cousin.

"I say, George - about Sir Henry Steere. I'm wondering where I heard his name before." George laughed, "Ho. Poor old Henry. Not a bad sort, really. From MI6 in London and then Wall Street: you know, a typical City man. He desperately wanted to become joint master of foxhounds, so we finally got old Clarissa to step down recently. Actually, she was past it after her fall – and old Henry had been angling for this appointment ever since he came over from the UK 10 to 15 years ago."

"Doing what?"

"Something to do with his family's bank in New York," George said. He quickly looked around, and then said in a low voice. "Dad's always hinted that we shouldn't open an account there. You know, our old bank? I don't quite know why."

"That's it. But there's something else too," Charles wondered aloud. Then as they went towards the hall he saw Sir Henry at the foot of the main staircase, listening in on Lady Fiona's and Georgiana's conversation. As they approached, Sir Henry – who'd recovered from his earlier awkwardness – said, "Ah, Charles. What are your plans for tomorrow?"

"Actually, I'm very much looking forward to George's lawn meet."

"Good. We're all of us going, you know. Aren't we George?" Lady Fiona turned round. "Henry, darling, you'll be so tired tomorrow morning. Do you think you should?" Her husband, however, chose not to hear. "That's settled, then." His leathery hand shook Charles's hand vigorously.

"Goodnight," he said heartily, again avoiding eye contact with Charles. "Goodnight," Charles replied, trying to get rid of his uneasy feeling. "Goodnight, George. See you at the usual time."

Sir Henry, unlike many of the more senior guests who were already leaving through the hall door, went towards the cloakroom with Fiona and Caroline. Others were starting to wish for their second wind, reduced as they were to sitting on the hard antique hall chairs and jealously eyeing the youth and vigour around them. The majority of guests had left but some stayed on, hopelessly determined to see in the dawn.

"In my day, you young thing, you … I shouldn't have been found talking to an old chap like me." Senator Cecil Gordonston-Lafitte spoke with relish as he sent off a young girl with an encouraging smack on her frock. "By Jove, He– therington," he continued, squatting down on the staircase beside his equally old friend. "They do turn them out now, don't they, what? Look at those fetlocks."

"I d… d… don't know, Cecil…" his companion stuttered, "But those young fillies d… d… don't really d… d… do anything to me any more."

"You're past it, old chap. We're all really past it, you know. Although, by Jove, remember your brother last year? What? What was the name of that girl?" Hetherington felt uncomfortable as Cecil continued to gently tease him. "The old cad. I'll never forgive him for it," Hetherington continued, having suddenly lost his stammer.

Standing some distance away towards the main hall staircase was Dr Caroline Conolly-Lafitte with her fine aquiline features topped with dark auburn hair, which was still full and bouncy in spite of the many hours of dancing. She was fondly watching Charles's reflection in the glass of a pastel painting as he kissed Marie goodnight – and then he moved the edge of his hand underneath his chin in the French manner while he crossed the hall leading to the main staircase to go to bed.

Charles looked at Caroline again as she stood examining a huge pastel painting of gigantic sunflowers by the Belgian artist Magrittte de Champs. As she'd turned to greet him her beauty softened as she smiled warmly. "Charles. How nice to see you again. I'm just about to leave, actually. Just waiting for the keys of my car …"

"Caroline?" he queried gently. "You're not driving alone at this time of the morning, are you?"

"Our place is only a mile away. I'm sure Annabelle's already gone on."

"I won't allow you to," Charles said firmly.

She looked into his kind eyes then beyond him through the inner glass doors of the hallway and beyond, out into the darkness outside. "You'll have to drive me then, won't you?" she said. She instantly wished she hadn't challenged him. "I shall certainly escort you," he volunteered, as he took the keys from the weary-eyed hall boy who was coming out from the back hall.

Caroline realised it was too late to start protesting now, as they were already moving towards the hall door. In turmoil at inconveniencing him she whispered desperately, "Charles?" But he was too busy asking the boy if he could drive, so he did not hear her. "Charles?" She pleaded with him softly again to reconsider.

* * *

Sir Henry Steere, who'd been observing Charles's tentative friendships all night, was lurking behind one of the marble columns in the hall. He watched them leave through the front door and then quickly crossed the hall before walking into the deserted, dark library. He switched on the lights and locked the library door of the now-empty room. He grabbed hold of the old rickety mahogany library stairs on wheels and pulled them alongside the middle of the long bookcase. After locking its wheels he climbed high up to the very top rung of the rickety staircase before making a calculated choice.

Yes. How appropriate. This is the very one he'd in mind. "It'll do nicely," he thought … No, the very thing … A large, hardbound copy of Cecil Aldin's hunting prints. He pulled it out and opened it up. Yes. Very distinctive. All individually coloured and signed. He closed the large book again, putting it partially back – and carefully noted its exact position (clearly jutting out from the top shelf) before climbing down again. Then he pressed down the brass double latch located just below the brand name Ladder-on-Wheels 1850, locking the tall mobile stairs into his selected position.

He looked up again directly at his chosen book and sighed heavily, thinking, "Perhaps a good parting present for my dear friend, after all." After he'd turned off the lights and walked out he closed the door gently behind him, looking left to right as he entered the hall again – then stopped and quickly turned fully around and locked the library door.

"Darling, there you are," he said to his wife, whom he found waiting outside the cloakroom. "Those old mahogany chairs are hard," he said to her. His new young wife looked up doubtfully and replied uneasily, "Whatever have you been up to, Harry?"

"Never you mind, my dear," brushing his lips against her cheek. "You'd never guess how many secrets old warriors like me still have to preserve. So very many, darling. Will I ever have enough time to tell you all of them?

Chapter Thirty-Three

B efore leaving the house Charles beckoned the hall boy to join them with a smile. "Here's a chance for you to drive a car." Then he handed the keys to the boy, who smiled from ear to ear. "Thank you, sir," he said, conscious that he was now one step up from being a simple tractor driver or hall attendant. Caroline observed Charles and the hall boy carefully making their way down the iced granite steps at the front of Gordonston Court. It was freezing, but it was not for warmth that Caroline felt herself being drawn to Charles: it was the quality of his silence and his grit as he made his tortured way down those slippery granite steps.

They were quietly happy as the hall boy drove the Jeep down the long winding avenue. It seemed endless, and only when they heard the rattle of the cattle grid at the gate did she turn to Charles. "We're the next entrance on the right," she smiled. "You did say you only lived a mile away."

"We do, taking into account both avenues. We're neighbours, actually." She smiled and told the hall boy, "We're the next entrance on the right. Here."

The powerful headlights swung in between the monumental granite pillars of the entrance gates, illuminating the broad avenue. On and on it went, over a bridge, through a leafless forest, before rising up again over fenced rolling parkland and horse country. Eventually more parkland with its mature bare oaks, sycamores and beeches came into view. In the distance Charles saw the vague outline of a mansion, with only a small fanlight illuminating its portico.

"Wait here," said Charles, addressing the hall boy as they arrived. "I won't be long." Then he and Caroline made their way to the main door, which was not locked. Caroline whispered, "Come in, Charles. Mummy and Daddy think I'm mad sleeping here on my own with Cousin Annabelle."

"I've no doubt you both are."

"Shh … you'll wake up Mr and Mrs Dean, the caretakers." Charles followed her through the black and white flagstoned hall. The celadon green wall colours continued along a corridor leading into the blazer-red library, where she switched on a tall reading lamp.

Ignoring the new digital disc player, she walked over to the adjoining conservatory. There she chose some dust-covered record sleeves that lay abandoned underneath one of the low window seats. Blowing away the dust from the records and placing two of them on an old gramophone player she blew on the aged needle and whispered, "I haven't played these records for at least 10 years. They're ancient, but I simply love Daddy's collection of Edith Piaf." She said this with the excitement of a young girl in her voice, and tugged off her dancing shoes. In her stockinged feet she appeared even more petite and fragile. She rolled up a section of the carpet, revealing a clear section of old parquet flooring.

Caroline looked at Charles fleetingly as Piaf's earthy Parisian music filled the room. Without a word she slipped silently into his arms, while she took one of his aluminium crutches from him and placed it under her right arm.

The golden light from the tall lamp drew colour from the burgundy-coloured walls and from the great variety of multicoloured books that were housed in the off-white library frames, which reflected the design of the three tall Georgian windows opposite. They both became one long shadow on the parquet floor as they danced: their silence above the music became more significant. She felt his chest expanding as she flicked her hair, a dark auburn mass, against his neck. Then she threw back her head, allowing her eyes to meet his.

She held her breath at the sharp click of the gramophone player, followed by a swoosh and a flap as the second record fell down. She observed their reflection in the bevelled panes of glass of the French windows of the double door to the conservatory, then looked up into his face again. Her small teeth glistened as her lips parted with a smile of wonder and satisfaction, then she lay her forehead against his chest and sighed like a child.

As they danced the deep, soulful music became part of them and she felt the comfort of his body against hers. Deep within she sensed the stirring of a beautiful world which she knew, someday, she would happily embrace. Her limbs seemed somehow to free themselves, becoming light and frail, until all strength in them seemed to vanish. A sensation of movement and freedom seemed to possess her and an overwhelming warmth enfolded her. Lifting her mouth she tried to whisper to him, but already his lips were on hers. She felt a very light, tingling sensation: it became deeper and warmer and Caroline felt that she never wanted that feeling to stop. Slowly, she rolled her face away from his just as the music stopped.

"Charles, you'd better take my car," she whispered. "I intend to fly back to Bogota after the hunt tomorrow and am being driven to the airport. Goodness me. Look at the time. It's past three in the morning."

"Oh, Caroline, I do hope we can make some time to discuss my mother's poem, which my father told me last week he discussed recently with you."

As they made their way to the front hall again she said in a low voice, "Yes. I thought it simply wonderful. I expect to be in

Geneva for a conference at the end of the year, but apart from that I won't see you for some time … but we can write to each other. At least you'll see Cousin Annabelle after the hunt, if she decides to stay on. I do hope she'll manage without your Arab."

"I'm glad she told you about Uncle Jacques's wonderful gift," he replied, amazed at Caroline's generous spirit and gentleness of heart.

"Goodnight," she whispered after him, watching him swing himself to the car. He turned and stood looking at her in the pouring rain and blew her a kiss. Her heart leapt as she realised at once the significance of that simple gesture. Had she'd finally met her soulmate? She'd found out who he was … how they both were, and were prepared to accept each other for what they each had become. "Thank you, God," she whispered to herself.

In spite of the freezing night she continued to hold the hall door ajar – and she kept on praying, watching and shivering as she waved … until the rear lights of the car finally disappeared. Then she closed the oak door, sliding the long flat metal bar into its 18th-century security socket.

Reflecting that someone else more than 300 years ago had stood here on this same cold spot, she wondered happily if that person had ever felt the same kind of feeling and warmth – and had hoped, like her, that it would never, ever go away. "*Que sera, sera*. Whatever will be, will be," she sang quietly through the door after him … adding softly, "May God bless you and keep you safe always, dearest Charles."

Chapter Thirty-Four

T hrough his long lens camera Il Terzina (the Oxford tourist) watched a tiny-waisted waitress at Brown's restaurant escort two men to join Anne at her table behind one of the three windows that fronted the Woodstock Road. The restaurant bustled with activity as Il Terzina watched Jean-Pierre embrace his wife, then waited as he saw him introduce his former tutor to her.

"Perfect." The assassin's eyes sparkled, reflecting his thoughts. Then he looked behind him at the yew-planted graveyard adjoining St Giles Church across the road from Brown's. "Not enough cover," he thought, and looked hopefully at the church's tower. "Angle too steep," he thought. As he looked to his right at the row of shops and fast food restaurant facing Brown's he concluded that the angle and location of the first floor windows of the Chinese takeaway would suit his needs perfectly. Then he went inside the ancient St Giles Church, to reflect calmly on his murderous plan.

* * *

"Brown's is still so full of character." Jean-Pierre turned to compliment his old tutor, who'd suggested it. "I love the bentwood chairs," said the other. "Brown's has, for many years now, captured the perfect balance between imaginative food and decent prices." The Oxford don spoke with a self-satisfied air, and continued with the same air. "For the more gourmet types among us there used, of course, to be the Elizabeth or the Sorbonne. But, alas, no more – Although the

Old Parsonage's kitchens have improved remarkably – had a gamy partridge there, recently." He grinned as he continued, "But you must be my guest at High Table at my college next time you're both in England." He said this in a manner known to everyone as being one of those Oxford invitations that were always handed out but seldom bore actual fruit. "But I think Anne must have magical powers to have secured this window table," he concluded. "Pot luck, I'm afraid," Anne said modestly.

For the next few minutes they examined each item of the menu while some garlic bread and three side salads were laid in front of them.

"Jean-Pierre, let's book you in for that lecture. I know you're busy at the bank but I'm sure you could manage to squeeze in just one talk … say sometime late next year?" Jean-Pierre stole a glance at Anne, who returned his look with a smile and a nod as she dipped into her salad. "Let's see now …" The pages of both men's diaries were flicking backwards and forwards when suddenly a sharp, cracking glass sound sent Anne rocketing off her chair. The first bullet sliced apart her face.

* * *

Il Terzina observed the carnage through his sights from one of the small top windows of the Chinese restaurant across the road from Brown's as scraps of brains and blood were sprayed around the glass alcove of Brown's. Il Terzina's right eye was still in the black rubber cup of the Zeiss scope as he pulled his trigger again, catching Jean-Pierre in profile on his knees tending to his wife's impossible wounds. Brown's's large restaurant window slowly crumbled with the second bullet, and the bustling waitresses froze in horror until the last tinkle of glass came to rest.

Then pandemonium broke out. Il Terzina quickly disassembled his light Italian rifle with its silencer and put it back into his tourist rucksack next to the yellow squash racket. He flushed the lavatory of the Chinese café before nonchalantly descending the stairs. Walking calmly around the corner at the Mannering shop, he passed the ancient church and walked along the stone path of its small church yard. Then he crossed the Banbury Road at the traffic lights, went down Keble Road and turned right at Keble College before confidently striding back to the corner pub near Blackwell's bookshop. He spied his triplet's green hired van awaiting him near the Kings Arms just as he approached Broad Street.

They did not speak, and celebrated only when they reached their aircraft at Oxford Airport in Kidlington. "Mission accomplished. Ireland here we come," they both shouted, and hugged each other.

Chapter Thirty-Five

As Cook arrived downstairs to take possession of her quarters early that Sunday morning at Gordonston House in Kentucky, no one else had yet stirred. She stopped momentarily on the stairs to listen to the unfamiliar sound of a helicopter, somehow conscious that she'd heard that same whine several weeks before. It would be some time before the house guests rose other than those members of the Gordonston-Lafitte family who complied with their duty to attend the 9.30 a.m. Sunday Mass in the house chapel. Already the birds were busily re-establishing their territories with song, but with no hint yet of morning sun it would be some time before the dew would begin to melt. Imperceptibly the gentle rumblings of country life began to make themselves felt as slowly the large mansion began to breathe normally.

This year, more guests than ever from neighbouring states had brought their mounts with them for George's Sunday lawn meet, filling all the available stabling and making full use of the adjoining empty hay stores.

*   *   *

At 10 a.m. a tally-ho could be heard coming from one of the larger farmhouses off the back avenue. The professional huntsman of the Gordonston hounds, Colonel Hetherington, woke himself up with his usual rousing start. Standing in front of the open window he now judiciously sniffed the frosted air again and, eyeing an overcast sky with a filtering sun, decided that it would be a good scenting day.

He quickly slipped on his ivory-coloured breeches and scarlet hunting jacket before walking a short way down the landing. He gave one sharp knock on his daughter's bedroom door, counted three, then gave two further raps before retiring back to his bathroom to complete his ablutions. This was the set routine and it never failed to rouse Rose, the first whipper-in. She was a very well-developed girl of 18, already tending to take after her mother - for whom every diet known to mankind had been unsuccessful. But that lady had a generous disposition – one that matched her physical size and which, with good humour, she had passed on to her equally generous daughter.

When Rose eventually came out of her room she was looking smart in her scarlet high-buttoned hunting coat. She accompanied her father down to the kennels to meet up with Will, the second whipper-in.

"Yert, Yert." The Irish lad drafted the selected hounds into two separate kennels. "All on, Miss Rose," Will said proudly. The restless hounds would not stop singing until they were poured into the hound van. This wouldn't take place until the large trucks containing the hunt servant's horses and those of the joint master and his wife, Sir Henry and Lady Fiona, were ready to depart a half-hour hour later.

* * *

In a nearby larger farmhouse Sir Henry Steere was still in bed, but his eyes were already open. He'd not been able to sleep for several hours after he'd come back from the ball: the scene of the intended murder of his best friend Cecil had been dominant in his mind. It had all been so carefully planned – and yet all he could now see were the difficulties as he lay there tossing from left to right, perspiring and yet feeling bitterly cold – as if the members of his body were continually falling off as in a dream.

Time and again he had shouted out in his nightmare, sitting up with a start as he tried to re-establish the few solid facts from his dream. Not the chocolate mobile staircase – which seemed to want to dance and move about, as it had also started to melt … and was incapable now of supporting even the weight of the single shoe which he had exchanged with the smaller shoe of his secret girlfriend. His mind too was getting hot. Perhaps some ice cubes or lubricating oils were required. "Be careful, Henry. You might spill it. There. We've no more sandpaper left." … Screams and howlings … until his mind had seized up – and so, intermittently, he slept.

But now his eyes remained open. All the possible scenarios of failure presented themselves to him. Enough. No more. With that thought he jumped out of bed. He ran the shower, scrubbed himself clean and shaved. No aftershave today, he decided – and carefully started to dress, taking it very slowly until he had fully recovered himself.

It'd been a bad night. It had been two whole days and one week since Sir Henry had officially retired from the family bank. He had to smile at the way he'd arranged it all. What better excuse than the taking up of his official duties as joint master? That would be his focus from now on. He would concentrate on this public duty first, and then the other assassinations – the main business – would no doubt take care of itself. He pottered about for a time with the map of the hunt and then, to kill time, he decided to put on his dressing gown and go down stairs and see whether he could find Minnie, who combined the duties of cook and parlourmaid. But he encountered total silence downstairs. He felt suddenly tired and went back upstairs to his dressing room. He lay down on the day bed, and so he fell asleep at last.

* * *

When Minnie the parlourmaid came in at 10 minutes past 10 with the breakfast tray and fixture card she was surprised to see Sir Henry still slumped on his single daybed, and she made a loud coughing sound. Sir Henry sat up quickly and tried to recover himself.

"Minnie, I shall have a late breakfast downstairs today," he announced pompously, stepping jauntily forward across the room towards the girl, adding quickly, "But do bring in these things to Lady Fiona." Then, spotting the post, he said, "I say, only one letter? Oh, it's for Lady Fiona." He dropped it with a flush of annoyance and embarrassment, not recognising the handwriting from one of Fiona's many American admirers.

"Ah, wait. I shall have the fixtures card. Now let me see ... Good Lord, Minnie, is that the time?" ... and he ran his forefinger under his white moustache. Stepping still closer towards the girl, he consulted the watch the size of a kitchen clock, which lay full square on her ample bosom. "Is it 10.15?" he queried, awkwardly clicking his heels and ticking the glass of the clock, as if it was a weather vane. Minnie turned the instrument towards herself, screwing up her eyes wildly. "Yes, sir: 11 minutes past 10," she confirmed, puzzled at the joint master's behaviour. She picked up the breakfast tray again and went next door, into Lady Fiona's separate but adjoining bedroom.

With slow deliberation Sir Henry finished off his grooming in front of the full-length mirror, which stood in the middle of his dressing room. The 10 days he had spent in the country after officially retiring had only slightly filled out his hollow cheeks but they had reduced the nervous twitching of his shoulders to a more gentle, less angular movement. He suddenly thought how pleasant life was in the country and how generous country folk appeared to be. He put on his newly-tailored scarlet hunting coat, with the distinctive buttons of the joint master. He turned around several times, examining himself closely with narcissistic indulgence.

Then a pained look on his face suggested a wider appraisal. He thought again of the effect his duplicity would have - not only on his victims, but also on himself. Suddenly he froze into a defensive crouching position as he heard the rattle of china in his wife's bedroom along the passage. Motionless, his eyes stole guiltily towards the shaded looking glass where he perceived himself crouching, about to rear upwards like a wolf with bloodied fangs. Shrugging his shoulders, he picked up a hairbrush from the dresser and deftly smoothed his greyish-white locks. He stood up straight, jerking his chin up sharply. He clicked his heels, tucked his top hat with its special home-made guard under his arm, and marched into his young wife's bedroom for his morning kiss.

"Good morning, darling," he beamed as he touched her tanned forehead (he hoped not too paternally). "Did you have a good rest?" Lady Fiona's room, full of bright colours with frills and photographs on her writing table, was quite the opposite of his rather bare, army-style quarters. "Oh Henry, darling, must I really get up? It's so marvellously warm down here." She was barely discernible in the large four-poster, from which she yawned. Then, burying herself like a dormouse under waves of blankets and eiderdowns before popping up her pretty head again, she said, "I do hope Minnie hasn't been horrible and hidden all my clothes. But darling, you're already dressed? How perfectly efficient you are."

She continued to prattle with a childish directness, making him feel awkward and at a loss for words. Sir Henry, who had lost his wealthy first wife under mysterious conditions many years before when he was still the right side of 50, could not quite recall – if he ever knew – how to behave in situations such as these – with his wife of 21 babbling on merrily, not allowing him the time to answer a single question she had asked. His legal and army training, his stay at the Colonial Office, MI6 and his banking career all warranted a self-possession and a calculated poise of a totally different kind.

Completely forgetting about his earlier instructions to Minnie he was soon sitting on the side of Fiona's bed, opening his mouth wide for the last slice of toast and marmalade. "Darling, you are perfectly horrid. Look, you've polished off my breakfast," she teased. With that he awkwardly scrambled down from the four-poster, jerking his coat sharply against the small of his back. "Err … must go down now … Err … check with Hetherington about the hounds." Attempting, unsuccessfully this time, to plant another kiss with his marmalade-plastered lips on her forehead, he hurried off downstairs.

Fiona, spying the still-unopened letter from one of her admirers (which was half buried under her napkin on the tray), looked at it in amusement. "Lady Fiona Constance Hermione Steere." She repeated her names to herself over and over. As she didn't recognise the handwriting she'd impulsively thrown the unopened letter on her dressing table, climbed down from the four-poster and run to the landing, calling down, "Henry … Henry …"

"Yes, darling?" He looked up adoringly as he came into the hall. "Oh, Henry, do remind Hetherington about letting Harry go out on his promised hunt today … Harry's so sweet, and …"

"But … but, darling … he is only a pup. He's barely six months old. He won't be up to it," Sir Henry replied. He felt for the pup, but there were the hunt members' valid interests as well … but in the end he was worried about upsetting his newly-acquired wife.

"Oh, Henry darling, I promise. Honest." She waved her blonde hair about wildly and closed her eyes fervently. "I promise … cross my heart … that Harry really won't be a bother. He is so clever … Oh, it'll be such fun … and I shall carry him on my lap should he get tired." Sir Henry, whose better judgment would have him refuse firmly, gave in once more. "All right, darling. I shall ask Will to keep an eye on him." He attempted a smile, managing in the process to look positively grim, but instantly cheered up as he looked up and saw Fiona beaming with delight.

"Oh you are a perfect angel," she said, and rushed back to her room to dress, leaving Sir Henry staring at the vacant banisters regretting his snap decision. Worried, he went back to his study to continue his perusal of a map of the chosen hunting area, determined to avoid making a complete fool of himself. At the same time he wanted to ensure that he fully understood where the Mississippi run was located and ensure not to be around when the assassinations took place. He encircled the area with a red biro and put the map in his pocket.

"Ah." Sir Henry's face lit up, as only skeleton versions of the normally-thick Sunday papers were brought in. "Thank you, Minnie," he said, and proceeded to consult the financial news columns of the only paper in Kentucky that had managed to put a series of press releases together. This, in spite of the difficulties he and his syndicate had created. "Yes … oho … good … good." After he'd recognised his own press release he stopped his exultation in mid flight as he became aware that Minnie had come back and was silently standing in the doorway with a surprised expression on her face. He coughed, embarrassed at his display, and proceeded to sit down with an apparent weariness which translated itself into his voice, which was now very vague and laid back. "Minnie, you may go now. Don't forget to include the usual sandwiches with the crust cut off the sides – very important - and the usual hip flask for Lady Fiona."

The young girl, baffled at Sir Henry's strange behaviour, looked more than usually blank. Awkwardly, she curtsied and disappeared. Sir Henry leaned forward again and continued to read his own press release, accompanied by an outdated photograph showing him in his sixties. Then his face went white at the thought of the assassinations and he slumped back in his chair. He sat quite still, breathing fast but rhythmically.

"Really, there is nothing for me to worry about," he thought. Everything was going according to plan so far. No doubt the assassin was already in position across the river, directly opposite the Mississippi run ridge. But as he thought of his own pending actions he felt himself to be a prisoner of events, and he hated being a captive. He jumped up, squared his shoulders and walked over to his desk. He carefully folded the newspapers so that his press release could not but be read – and just to make sure, he rang for Minnie and gave her clear instructions. "Minnie, have this brought up to Gordonston Manor later on, before they start serving the stirrup cups."

With a sharp smack of his hunting whip against his leather boots he stalked outside down the farm avenue with grim determination on his face. The cry of hounds in the distance lightened his step, and he again assigned all murderous plans behind one of his many invisible Chinese walls for the time being.

He now thought only of a perfect day's hunting with his delightful new wife. With each step, however, he became more apprehensive at the sharply rising temperature, which was melting the frosty puddles – and turning them into muddy pools – which he tried to avoid so as not to stain his brightly-polished black hunting boots. "Probably good for the scent," he smirked sarcastically as he entered the kennel yard.

"Morning, Hetherington," he hailed, but the Colonel was reprimanding Will, the second whipper-in, who in turn was rather unnecessarily cracking his whip at the hounds, rating them familiarly by name as if he was reprimanding a pack of coolies.

Sir Henry coldly observed this, but started to laugh triumphantly. Everything was going according to plan. This was going to be the fox hunt of the season. "Capital," he shouted at the top of his voice, attempting thereby to throw off any internal scruples and scent of his lurid, evil intentions.

"Best not linger, just in case someone should read my thoughts about the pending assassinations on the Mississipi run," he thought, slinking away out of sight towards Gordonston Manor for his last stirrup cup with four more victims.